I0668308

The Story of Lucy Belmont

The Story of Lucy Belmont

LUISELLA TRAVERSI GUERRA

Translated by Margaret Louise Fitzgibbon

RESOURCE *Publications* · Eugene, Oregon

THE STORY OF LUCY BELMONT

Copyright © 2024 Luisella Traversi Guerra. All rights reserved. Except for
brief quotations in critical publications or reviews, no part of this book may be
reproduced in any manner without prior written permission from the publisher.
Write: Permissions, Wipf and Stock Publishers, 199 W. 8th Ave., Suite 3, Eugene, OR
97401.

Resource Publications
An Imprint of Wipf and Stock Publishers
199 W. 8th Ave., Suite 3
Eugene, OR 97401

www.wipfandstock.com

PAPERBACK ISBN: 979-8-3852-2360-2
HARDCOVER ISBN: 979-8-3852-2361-9
EBOOK ISBN: 979-8-3852-2362-6

06/26/24

Disclaimer:
This is a work of pure fiction. Any names or characters are fictitious, and any resemblance to actual persons, living or dead, or to any actual events or incidents, is purely coincidental. Any businesses or places described are either wholly fictional, or were inspired by distant memories, news stories, local history books, and local folklore the author came into contact with when writing the manuscript in 1999. Any descriptions or scenes involving these business or places are fictitious, any inaccuracies are due to a faulty memory, an overactive imagination, or the passage of time.

"Se esiste a Evansville un luogo per sognare,
possiamo allora sognare anche noi"
BENITO GUERRA

"If there is a place for dreaming in Evansville,
then we can dream too"
BENITO GUERRA

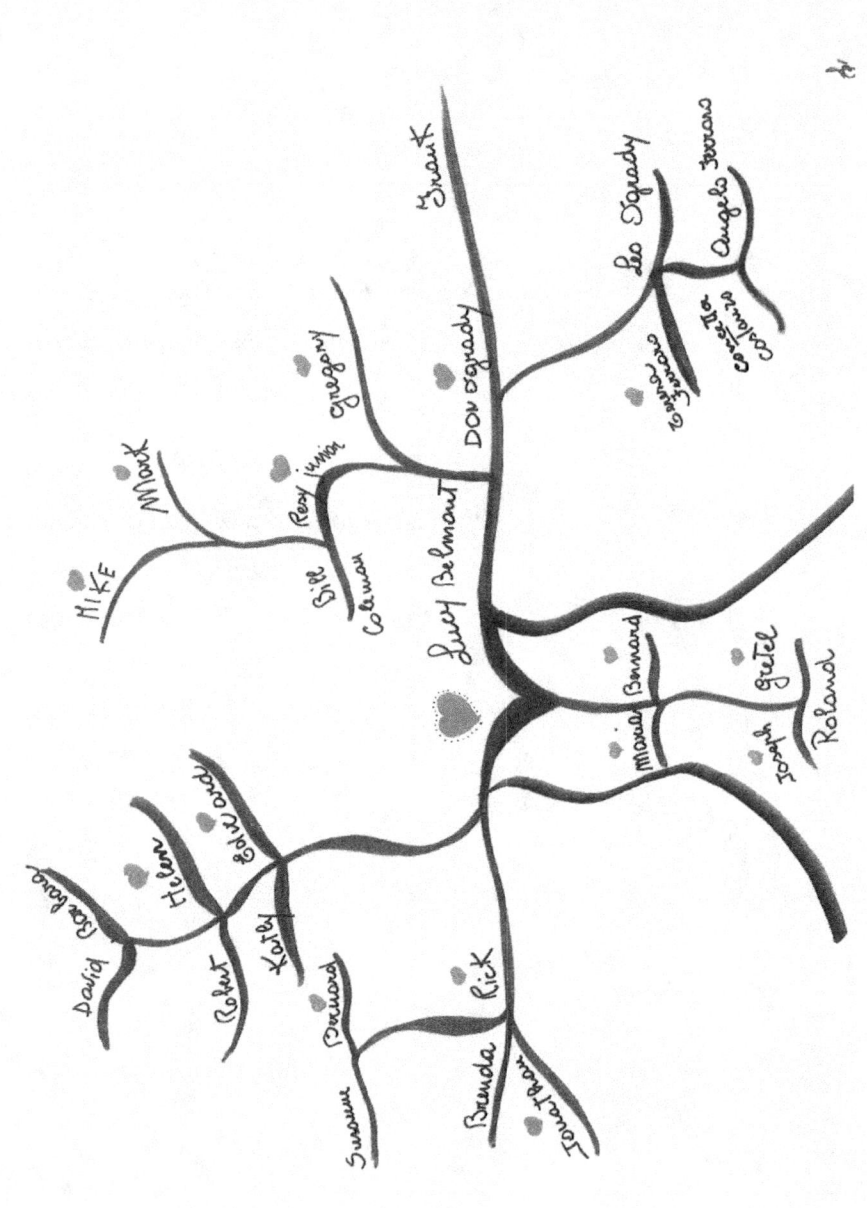

Author's note

I COMPLETED THIS MANUSCRIPT in late 1999, then hid it in a drawer for over two decades before deciding to publish it. I offer it to you exactly as it came to me, in a rush of angst and enthusiasm for the new millennium, complete with the original note below. I hope it conveys to you my emotional state as I wrote it in an unhindered flow, almost unconsciously including some autobiographical details in what was otherwise a work of pure fiction. It's a story with an old-fashioned feel to it, centered around the eternal question—what happens after we die? The setting is in the afterlife, suspended in a period of time which some might call the weighing of the soul, while the action takes place in the nebulous realm of memory. Does this really happen? Who can say—but isn't it worth pausing for a few moments of intense personal questioning, to imagine what might occur as the spirit detaches from the body and we depart from the physical world to take on a new and mysterious form of existence?

Our tale begins in Evansville, Indiana, a vibrant midwestern city bathed by the waters of the vast and majestic Ohio River. Its landscape is classic Corn Belt; an endless, dancing sea of grain and soy, sparsely dotted with the few islets of oak woods that remain. Statistically, Evansville is often rated as one of the best places in America to raise children due to the serene and stately pace of life there. About forty miles away lies the village of New Harmony, a fascinating gem of American architecture, which was a purpose-built utopian community modeled on the ideal of Paradise, as imagined by a group of German settlers in the early 1800s. These pious adventurers fervently believed that they could create their own heaven-on-earth on the beauteous and bountiful land they found.

Driving though this region, you immediately understand why. Your heart soars free in the boundless yet orderly empty spaces—a perfect playground for human creativity. I happened upon Evansville by pure chance, on business, yet I instantly, and intuitively felt that this part of America would come to mean a lot to me. It was 1990 when I first came, and indeed to this day I feel tied to the place by an undefinable sentiment. The experience of writing this short novel touched me profoundly, so much so that by the end of the process, I felt like the Evansville way of living had really become a part of me, and perhaps even suited me better than my native Italian lifestyle. After many years of coming and going, I finally achieved the pleasing and agreeable sensation of belonging to, and in, this place that I have grown to love.

As I said, this story is my invention, but it sprouted unexpectedly from a series of coincidences that made it feel especially real to me. In the late summer of 1999, while I was in Evansville with my husband, we heard that our dear friend Dan was in poor health, and so went to pay him a visit. Dan was laid up but in good spirits, and like always, he gave us the rundown of all the local gossip. Knowing I was an ardent admirer of historical Evansville, he told me that the fifth graders of the Hebron Elementary School had written a book all about their hometown and its rampant development over the past century; Green River Road—From Cornfields to Concrete. That same day, I headed straight to Barnes & Noble, the bookstore where I often spent my Sunday afternoons, to pick up a copy.

The conversation with Dan and his charming anecdotes had stimulated my curiosity, and I began to wander around the local history section. It was enchanting reading—the myriad stories of the fine old city, the stern ancestors staring out from their faded photographs, the transformation from log cabins to brick buildings, and from saloons to drive-ins and giant malls, all seemingly in the blink of an eye. As I perused the stirring images of the immigrants who had left Europe afflicted by poverty and deprivation to build their own paradise in the free world, I realized these were people who had had the guts to turn their lives upside down and bear countless hardships and humiliations in pursuit of a simple dream; a life of freedom and basic dignity. I bought several of those hauntingly beautiful books to help me better understand American values, perhaps even make them my own. I still regard those volumes as a treasure trove.

In the weeks that followed, I often found myself passing by Green River Road and Morgan Avenue, and each time I would stop and take a look at a particular old house on the corner lot that always caught my eye. Shuttered, mysterious and darkly intriguing, the deep front porch had somehow withstood the onslaught of time, smog and the constant nerve-rattling traffic. Beyond it the immense, still luscious garden lay abandoned and hopelessly overgrown—each of its tangled shadows and secret spaces whispering to me a different narration. From the lonesome, mummified remnants of that once handsome and well-loved home, this story took its first hazy form, only to condense and deepen, one tale dropping into another, shapeshifting like a Russian doll, and shedding layers of existence, until finally, I reached the nub of what it was all about; the essence, the dwelling place of the soul.

Perhaps it was the potent cocktail I imbibed from those fascinating books, or the strange beneficent energy that emanated from that old house, or my usual overactive imagination, or a mix of all three that led to this novel essentially writing itself. Whatever the reason, one morning, a few months after that pivotal chat with Dan, I awoke with a start, long before dawn, only to hear the voice of a well-spoken, elderly woman quite loudly pronounce the words: "My name is Lucy Belmont, I'm ninety-seven years old. I lived in the house on the corner of Green River Road and Morgan Avenue, I've been dead for three days, but nobody's noticed yet."

Bergamo, February 21, 2000.

CHAPTER 1

MY NAME IS LUCY Belmont and I'm ninety-seven years old. I've been dead for three days, but nobody's noticed yet. I've lived in this house almost all my life, on the corner of Green River Road and Morgan Avenue in Evansville, Indiana. Is anyone there? Can you hear me? I must talk to someone; there's so much I still don't understand . . . isn't anybody there at all?

I'm not sure where my story starts. To begin at the beginning would take too long, and I'm not sure how much time I have. Facts: I was born in 1903, in Saint Wendel, not far at all from Evansville itself. My mother, though fiercely proud of her Bavarian roots, was an American born and bred, while my father was a French immigrant who came here in the late 1890s. I believe I died three days ago, sitting in the old rocking chair in my bedroom, facing the window that looks east onto Green River. Why has nobody has come to check on me? Maybe it'll take the reek of my dear old bones rotting to attract some attention. Ha! That stubborn, unrelenting body that kept me company over the interminable years of my life will finally betray me. Perhaps someone will call Sheriff Hobson, and he'll come and kick open the back door, and tumble straight into the kitchen—I do hope I left it tidy.

But what am I saying? Where am I now? If I'm dead, how can I still be here, talking—I just don't understand! Where is everybody? I feel so light, it's like I'm floating. I can hear the clock ticking on my nightstand

and the whirr of the air conditioner, but I can't feel my gold chain anymore, the one with the little diamond that my Don gave me for our thirtieth anniversary. I love that necklace . . . or should I say I loved it? Every time I touched it, I felt happy. It laid against my breastbone like a warm palm, giving me strength, helping me make peace with whatever was going on around me. I was never a typical American beauty, but people said I had something unique, a touch of class, perhaps because of my French blood. My husband told me he'd fallen in love with my natural elegance, my poise—I had the airs and graces of a fine lady, he used to say half-jokingly. Needless to say, he didn't have much of a way with words.

That's why he decided to take me to Sears and buy me that necklace. It was December 14, 1959, I remember it like yesterday. It was a perfect afternoon. I remember how he looked at me, proud and attentive, as a smug salesgirl fastened the clasp around my neck. For a few eternal seconds, like never before and never since, I felt like I was the exact center of the universe and everything was spinning around me. To feel loved and seen that way by your own husband, after so many years of life together . . . it thrilled me. I felt as giddy as a schoolgirl, like I'd jumped back in time to the very day we first met, three whole decades ago, at the racetrack in Indianapolis. Who knows who'll be wearing my necklace from now on? Will it mean anything to them? Will they even like it, or will they just shove it in a drawer?

I've been dead for three days, but nobody's noticed yet—and I'm trying not to take offense. What a strange place this is. There's a soft, blurry light and a feeling of calm now, it's welcoming, cozy even. I don't see anybody, but I feel a warm embrace around me, and as it hugs me tighter, I feel like it's squeezing the words out of me, like I'm spilling over the rim of wherever I am, escaping. Maybe it's the rigor mortis setting in. I'd begun to think I might never die, that Death himself had forgotten all about me! Over the last few years, sitting on my front porch, I'd often catch myself wondering what it would be like when I passed away, but I never could have imagined I'd find myself here, just sort of stuck like this. I mean, I feel quite alright, I think it's all over—there's no rush at all as a matter of fact. I really just want to talk. I would quite like to set things straight, to neatly file away all my doubts, erase all my question marks. What would my tale be after all, without all my tribulations and triumphs, joys and secrets, all my silenced, wrinkled subterfuges.

Now that I actually take the time to think about it, I can see that my life really has been just like a river flowing. I know it's a cliché but it's also as true as steel and as plain as the nose on your face—so there it is. Right from when I sprung up in Saint Wendel, I've always felt the rippling in my blood. Year after year I learnt how to read the currents and the swells, how to traverse the rapids and the shallows without getting dragged under. I kept sight of where I was aiming to get to and started to recognize ahead of time where I would have to merge and dip. If you follow the law of the river, it will bear you up and bob you along, right through to the sea-mouth, or wherever it is you want to go. Studying the pale, placid waters of the Wabash, the Green and the Ohio, I learnt to ebb and flow, navigating obstacles while maintaining a superficial calm, never straying far from the path. Water that strays too far beyond the riverbed soon trickles away into nothing. I chose to navigate my existence as best I could, aiming midstream, for the no man's land. I made Evansville my hometown and lived there for the best part of a century. With little fuss, and as much dignity as I could muster.

Evansville started out a happy place I think, not too big or spread out, just a cluster of log cabins so fortuitously situated along a broad horseshoe curve of the great and grand Ohio River. We had our European origins in common, my comely home and I, and we understood each other instinctively. Evansville too had a unique air about it; its mostly Germanic community conserved a love of the old ways; an innate appreciation of fine craftsmanship, and a certain formality. There was often touch of grace in the details of its buildings in spite of how fast they sprang up, an honest beauty in the local clay bricks and unpretentious wrought iron railings, in the solid wooden gables hewn from the virgin hardwood forests that flourished all around. When I left our backwoods farmstead and came to live in Evansville, the fancy town center was already a modern marvel. The imposing brick courthouse, the Vanderburgh County jail, the beautiful Willard Library—they easily rivaled those of the big cities, or so I was told. The wealthy folk lived in great stone mansions with all manner of exotic wonders at their disposal; tapestries, carvings, chandeliers, velvet upholstery, even stained glass from France and marble fireplaces from Italy.

These noble residences richly adorned the sweeping avenues, and carriages went back and forth constantly, trotting the fashionable from one engagement to another. Despite such refinements, the most coveted jewels of my town, (and do let me say that to me it will always be a town, never a city), were the towering trees that lined the broad streets. Oaks, sycamores, elms, lindens, maples; kindly giants that cheered me through the seasons, waving and whispering, slow-waltzing in the caress of the river breezes. I absolutely love trees, and in Evansville they're everywhere of course—bursting from the parks and gardens or bunched up in gossipy little woods where you can find such pleasant shade in the summertime. I cannot describe to you the exquisite perfume of our apple orchards, nor the sheer perfection of the lindens standing straight in parallel ranks, like they were lined up for a cotillion. Fall's colors here are beyond ordinary words; saffron, ochre, amber, cerise, tangerine, titian, carmine, vermillion, ruby, russet . . . tiger-colored leaves aflame everywhere, the life in them so flagrant and palpable.

My name is Lucy Belmont, and once upon a time I was a school-teacher. I'm sorry if I'm repeating myself or talking out of turn. I'm not sure why, but I want you to know that I lived decently and kept up appearances right to the very last moment, in spite of everything. My thoughts come and go now, drifting gently like clouds, then suddenly all those leopard leaves start leaping about in my draughty dappled mind. What am I saying? Are all these rustling syllables my own or am I just reciting something? I've always kept my verses to myself, until now. I did like being around people, and I believed in being generous with my time, but I'm no stranger to solitude. Perhaps I should more rightly say it didn't much bother me until now, not even as a little girl, deep in the wilds of Saint Wendel where I was born.

How I loved the squirrels that played in the trees around my house, and the spotted turtles struggling through the long, wet grass. I loved the wide rivers that flowed through the vast green farmlands, the red and iridescent dusks—the way that hefty evening sun would somehow slip so deftly into undulating argentine waters of the Ohio. I loved the lofty trees reaching up into the clear blue, the lone clouds sailing fast and unfettered in the infinite space above. I was fascinated, and frightened, by the massive storms that came on like stampeding buffalo, threatening disaster. And of course, I loved the delicate wildflowers that magically appeared every May, sprinkling a thousand pretty colors over the fields and along the lanes. I always felt an odd stirring inside me when I saw the ducks in flight, high above me. It was as if their beating wings and hoarse, familiar cries were towing the coming season into being through sheer force, dragging it over my head like a blanket.

Born in such a place, it was natural for me to live in harmony with the changing seasons and their fine parade of colors, scents, and emotions. The sudden release of spring, opening in wonderment, the riotous dancing pulse of summer in the cornfields, the blazing spectacle of the fall foliage. Then came winter, which I loved most because it came so powerfully, imposing the slow steps and ponderous silence of deep snow. I loved to gaze out across the unbroken fields, the white horizon dissolving into the whiter sky, just breathing, and letting that serenity soak into me after one of life's unavoidable storms had passed. How could anyone feel lonely?

But I digress! I was born on a farm, not much more than a double log cabin and a barn with some livestock near the low rolling hills of Saint Wendel . . . have I said that already? Should I tell you about it? We were surrounded by woods of course. I remember like yesterday how my brothers and I used to play among the wide oaks, how we made up secret names for each of them, how we'd pretend we were lost and then ask them to point the way back to the cabin with their branches. Naturally, we were poor, but we didn't have any idea about that and ours was just like all the neighboring farmsteads, no worse, no better. As a matter of fact some backwoods folk didn't even have anything to farm and just got by on game and corndodgers. We wanted for nothing. Our generous land easily contented our little hearts and bellies, though it slowly wore out our parents and grandparents.

The best spot on our farm was the orchard when it blossomed, because the smell was so divine, and of course it magically produced all my favorite treats—apples, pears, peaches, cherries, plums, and much more. These were the ingredients for my grandmother's jellies and preserves, which were famous far and wide. Grandma said the secret of their special flavor was in the touch of lemon peel she added—it wasn't so easy to come by in those days. One day Mr. and Mrs. Owen, the grandchildren of the very founder of New Harmony no less, sent their cook to learn how she made her peach jelly. She was so flattered by the attention that she gave away all her secrets, right down to the tiniest detail, but they say it never turned out quite like Grandma's. Maybe because she put so much love into her work, or maybe because she had what Grandpa called that special *European* touch. My own Mama inherited some of her talent, and she used to make the best cherry pie you've ever tasted.

I do still love cherry pie, it's like a warm hug. Just a few days ago I asked Mary, my housekeeper, if she'd buy me a cherry pie. It might be defrosting now in the fridge as we speak. Dear God, please don't let them throw it away—I couldn't bear to see it go to waste!

CHAPTER 2

SHOULD I KEEP GOING? Is someone coming?

I'm burning to tell you everything, yet what is there really to tell? I'm low on chit-chat and out of practice. My life wasn't intense like my friend Amy Cox. She went all the way to Boston to study singing and ended up touring around America, from theater to theater. Whenever she was home to visit her folks, we would get together and catch up. She used to tell me all about her adventures in California, Virginia, and even New York City. Listening to her wild tales make me feel funny somehow. I was fascinated, a little bitter, and even oddly nostalgic for those grand places I'd never actually been to, but that unsettled feeling her talk gave me didn't sit well with me, and deep down I preferred my quiet life to her fast-moving one. Amy used to end her stories with a big laughing sigh, "but maybe you're more content than me," she'd say. She was right: back then I truly did possess the gift of serenity, though I wasn't conscious of it. Just a few years later, when my family started to hit trouble, only then did I realize how rare and valuable my inner stillness was, and how its strength could suddenly spring up. Sometimes, that kind of stillness can be radiant, radiant enough to placate and even to purify us—if we let it.

In the house where I was born lived my maternal grandparents, my parents, and my three older brothers Jonathan, Rick, and Edward. I was the little mascot of the family, and the apple of my father Bernard's eye. I was the only girl, and I was the only one who took the trouble to learn a little French from my Papa, as well as some German from my grandparents. I was a bright child and I adored going to school. My father often spoke to me of his native France, of Pas de Calais. He told me stories of how the mountains of the north were made by the hands of his people, from the very rubble and stones they had hauled out of the mines. His home was a rainy hamlet in Avion, where every August there would be a merry village fete and apparently everyone knew how to play the accordion and sing like a lark. Though he just played by ear, Papa could play very well, and it was one of the few possessions he brought with him when he left home, on his great voyage to the promised land of America.

Many years later, I gave that old accordion to my son Greg. I often wonder if that's where his love of music came from. Like Papa, he had a natural talent and learned fast. I remember how his music would always draw a smile or a tear from me, sometimes both! I always was a big softy. On the long warm summer evenings, when he and his friends would sit out on the back porch, I would sit listening to him play through the open kitchen window, letting waves of emotions pass through me, feeling sheepish and silly, and fortunate. Greg had a fine voice, too, and played several instruments, but it was the accordion that he was most attached to, it was like a direct line between grandfather and grandson—their own special language, though they never actually met.

For my Papa growing up, the distant dream of America was a dream of the future. He longed for the chance to swap his dreary life as a miner for the more dynamic prospects of a ranch hand or a laborer building the railways and canals of a far-off continent where anything was possible for a young man unafraid of hard work. He loved to tell the tale of how, after many sacrifices, his parents managed to put together the price of his passage, and he finally embarked at Calais, heading to England. He would never see his mother or father again. Overcoming a multitude of challenges, he eventually reached America via Liverpool, having found himself a position as a cabin boy on an ocean liner.

During the long winter evenings in the log cabin, Papa would recount endless snippets of his odyssey; his sleepless nights due to rough seas or the fear of rats, the times he took refuge up on deck, surrounded by black water and nothingness on all sides, bolstering his courage by picturing himself as Christopher Columbus off to conquer the New

World. One night, with clear skies and a full moon, he even saw a gam of whales not far from the ship. It was one of my favorite stories, and I would demand to hear it over and over again. For many years he kept a drawing I made for him as a little girl—it was he and I, the moon and the ship, floating in a sea of spurting whales and whizzing stars.

Papa was not very robust, but like all true Frenchmen he loved a glass of wine in good company, and he was an avid storyteller. My timid mother, Maria, was almost put off by his overt friendliness, but his gentle spirit took such a strong grip on her heart that she eventually gave in and agreed to marry him. Mama's people had come over from Bavaria, in Germany, but she was a child of the New World. Thinking back, I can't imagine how she persuaded her stern parents to welcome him as their son-in-law. Fervent Catholics, Josef and Gretel had immigrated with a large group of settlers all from the same religious community, determined to begin a new life, free of sin and devoted to spirituality. It seems that at the time, the old continent had become a burden to many people. Poverty, unemployment, corruption, the semi-serfdom many still endured even if in more modern guises, these were all factors that pushed the more enterprising youngsters to tempt fortune and try to carve out a new way of life overseas.

I'll never forget how my grandparents, even in the most trying times, would repeat to us children how lucky we were, how extraordinary life was in this new land that had welcomed them, how blessed and how free we were here. America meant just that to my family—freedom. Freedom, of course, meant dignity, independence, liberty from the caste of low birth and the tyranny of the ancient ruling families of their homeland, in a fresh and bountiful paradise just waiting to be discovered. The land their community settled on and slowly tamed was indeed a paradise, a rolling countryside of oaks, persimmons, sassafras, sugar trees, hackberry and, of course, massive acacia groves—a sure sign of the fertility of the terrain. It was populated with all manner of God's creatures, from familiar-looking deer, hogs, and wild turkeys to strangely patterned snakes, bright green parakeets and flame-red cardinals. Rivers full of fish, trees full of fruit, good land, good hunting, good lumber—to those frugal peasants used to the taxes and trials of the old continent, such unplundered, virgin territory was simply heaven.

We children didn't understand the older generation, of course. For us America was our daily bread, the air in our lungs and the blood in our veins—the cabin, the woods, the animals, the very soil we worked with our bare hands and walked with our bare feet. It was hard living by today's standards, but it was a happy, bucolic, abundant place nonetheless. We took it for granted because we knew nothing else, and we loved it sincerely, and felt sure that it loved us in return. I still clearly remember lying back in the tall grass of our feather-soft meadows and feeling the very earth itself embrace me; I miss that fragrant, hugging warmth like a favorite aunt. I was an integral part of our land, we were all of one blood, an extended family. That land grew our food, grew our flesh and bones, grew even the trees our house was made of. Our well water sprang out of that land and we drank it, and bathed in it; we were one inseparable organism.

My infancy was full of lessons and blessings. My family gave me two stable foundation stones on which to build my character through daily practice: gratitude and serenity. In good times and in bad, these pillars have always been my solace. My grandparents attempted to pass on all their Bavarian traditions to me, but I only ever wanted to hear their curious tales of the Alps. Those massive mountains, they said, were full of magic and wonder. They would turn red and purple at sunset and were covered in trees so thick you could get lost and never find your way out, even if you walked for weeks on end. They often told me the tale of my great-grandfather, Roland, who went out hunting in a place the locals called "the labyrinth," and went missing for more than a month. Then they would unravel an elaborate yarn about how he survived by eating wild berries and mushrooms, mingled with forest creatures both kind and fierce, and eventually befriended a stag with golden antlers who showed him the way out of the woods. After that adventure, they said, my great grandfather always kept a pair of antlers hanging over his fireplace, symbols of the blessings he had received; good luck, and mercy.

When Grandpa Josef left his parent's home in Bavaria, Great-Grandpa Roland gave him his own blessing under the antlers; that his values would always guide his steps until he, too, found his path in life. Religion was the center of my grandparent's lives, and this was a given for them, they had no concept of any other way of living. They had a wooden crucifix up on the wall, and my grandmother was very attached to it, as it had been handed down through the females of her family for generations. She would often say it was at least three hundred years old, though I don't recall how she counted back so far. It certainly did look ancient though. On rare occasions she would take it down to give it a good clean, and sometimes she would let me hold it. I seem to recall it was as hard and heavy as stone, and I had to keep it tight to my chest and grip it with two hands. Every evening before supper, as we recited our prayers, I would sneak a glance at Grandma, who would be staring at it, lovingly bewitched by her crucifix. Her eyes shone, her faith so forceful—that cross gave her just as much strength as Jesus and the saints turning up at the dinner table would have done. She emanated conviction, and we all felt somehow protected, sacred, and safe near her.

Whenever we kids would get up to mischief, she was the one to go to for confessions and comfort, knowing that hers was a tender, nearby God that would never actually punish us much. Eventually that crucifix, along with part of the cabin itself, was destroyed in fire. We felt the loss of it almost as keenly as the damage to our home, as if we had suddenly been orphaned, bereft of our benevolent domestic deity. We rebuilt, and made a new wooden cross, but it was never the same. Somehow, I think Grandma's adoring glances had infused the old one with so much love that it used to shine back at us whenever we looked at it. My grandparents passed on their love of God to all of us children, etched it into us so deeply that not even the crudest stabs of destiny could erase it. I, Lucy Belmont, right to my final moment, have always believed that there is good in every creature, simply because we are all creations of God. My husband used to joke about it, saying I would never grow up, never stop believing in fairytales, but I knew that deep inside me there was, and still is, a deep well of love that can never run dry.

Even now, all I need to do is picture the sun setting, the ducks beating their wings, the flowers in my garden blooming, and soon I feel the water flowing and my well filling up again. I can feel it distinctly: the rippling hum of nature. I am part of the greater harmony, the universal rhythm which joins all the world's wonders together. My faith taught me early on that the meaning of life cannot always be revealed in concrete, visible things. Sometimes, rather often actually, we find it hiding in intangible sensations. It insinuates itself into our beings almost imperceptibly, like ivy spreading on our shadiest walls. This miniscule, prickly, furtive visitor, if welcomed, can open the eyes of our secret soul. Only its tiny barbs can pick the lock, a lock that can only be opened from the inside, and which lays the truth of ourselves bare.

CHAPTER 3

WHAT IS THIS PLACE? Am I really dead and gone, or still just coming and going? I feel so light and free, no more aches and pains. That niggling in the spine I used to get as I sat for hours staring out the bedroom window is gone. Behind the yellowing curtains, my bored eyeballs drying out, I'd play spot the pedestrian, hoping most of all for a familiar face . . . but nowadays hardly anyone comes this way on foot. How different it was when I was a girl! Evansville was a bustling community, and the streets were continually crisscrossed by all manner of traffic; people, bicycles, horses, mules, stagecoaches, buggies, and crowded wagons. Sometimes the passengers' faces were so caked in road dust that they could just as well have been Egyptian mummies. Men would ride into main street to do business, but in actual fact spend far more time dawdling with the garish women who worked in the saloons that were springing up everywhere. My folks referred to them abstractly as "ladies of leisure," telling me to look away in order to preserve my innocence when we were in town.

Thus, to my childish eyes, every saloon became a place of great mystery. Whenever I happened nearby one, I felt myself being sucked in by curiosity, and at the same time repulsed by a vague sense of guilt or embarrassment. When I tried to imagine what was going on inside, I pictured one of these painted ladies turning and looking down towards me, her crooked red mouth an open gash, her bawdy laughter the squawking of a crow. I tried to steal glances in through the doors, but a mist of fear descended, so the clinking glasses and bustling waiters seemed to me like noise coming from a hidden cellar. Each time the doors swung outwards, the saloon exhaled a heavy sigh of something sour and imprecise—wet straw, acrid sweat, loose morals, things that leave a stain—and off I would scurry, worrying confusedly about my clean smock or some such. My brothers had no such fears, of course, and would stand about outside, gawping until they were shooed away by a grown-up. I just didn't have the gumption; if I ever broke a rule or told the slightest half-truth, I was riddled with guilt. You could tell early on that I was destined for a quiet, predictable existence.

I can hardly believe it now, that fluttery little girl so bamboozled by town life, by saloon doors and fair rides, by rodeos and brass bands, and this ancient creature planted in her chair—how can they both still be me, one in the same, Lucy? Could that tiny sapling really have meta-morphosized into this gnarled, hollow Evansville oak? No more buds for me now, no more acorns, no more bright colors; I seem to feel the loosening in the stems of my last curling leaves. It's like one hand letting go of another, an elderly couple at the end of their long walk. Or maybe not a couple, maybe a just an old woman who has finished her prayers, intertwined fingers releasing each other as she slowly rises. Perhaps all I'm waiting for is the descent of those last leaves, perhaps when they touch the ground I'll disappear.

Am I rambling again? What I mean to say is this: the long years of my life, the world around me babbling relentlessly from an archaic land-bound subsistence right up to the electronic simulation of life that I met with at the end—what has it meant? A life, this modern life with its endless tangle of technological sophistications but none of the smell or the flavor it used to have, is this really what we were put here for? My beloved radio, my telephone, the television that became both lifeline and ball and chain—was the TV screen the only warm glow of my last years?

Those things were supposed to keep me in touch with the world and with my loved ones, my far-flung children, my relatives and friends, but did they? Or, instead, did they soften me up, fool me into letting go of the reins, lengthening the leash, slackening the bonds of familiarity until they all faded into the distance? Why did we spread out so much when all we really ever had was each other? I could see anything I wanted in virtual world of television, share my existence with my loved ones through the cold touch of a receiver, their disjointed voices coming and going. Yet I was less certain year by year whether the voices on the other end of the line were real or imagined; I lost track of who had died and who had just moved away, of whether the callers were reaching me from the other side of the globe or perhaps from the afterlife? How does any of this business actually work, this magic made with wires and cables? For all I knew, my loved ones had been miniaturized and trapped in the plastic handset by an evil genie.

For what it was worth, I tried to keep in step with the times for as long as I could. I thought it was the right thing to do, to make a deliberate effort not to become a crazy old bat. I kept on working, volunteering, reading, thinking, trying to be a part of things for as long as I could. In her later years, even my own mother ventured out into the world, taking brief trips to see the wonders of the big cities like Chicago and New York, so she, too, slowly evolved and acclimatized to life in the twentieth century. Grandma Gretel, however, never wandered far from the farmstead and never changed a bit. Rather, she was like a living photograph of the late 1800s, still enveloped in her long, dark dresses even as the flapper style of the Roaring Twenties was sweeping in. Who lived best?

CHAPTER 4

My name is Lucy Belmont, and I've been stuck here for quite a while now. Isn't anybody coming? I've tried shouting, but no one hears me. I'm not even sure if I'm talking out loud or in my head.

I clearly remember the first time I overheard my parents arguing about my eldest brother Jonathan. He had started keeping bad company and was even refusing to go to church with us anymore. His new friends were mostly out-of-towners who would blow into Evansville on whatever their business supposedly was, and he would immediately drop everything to fall in with them. In those days the town port had become a hub for paddle steamers, which you could often see carrying intrepid travelers up and down the Ohio River, alongside the usual flatboats laden with cottons, tallow, molasses, flaxseed oil, nails, rope—anything you could trade. You could go all the way to Saint Louis, Missouri. To us simple farmers it was an almost mythological place; the big city, the door to the West. On the wagons headed to the river port, you could meet persons of every origin and extraction. There were some ruthless adventurers among them, eager to prey on the ingenuous farm boys and ranch hands out looking for a better life. I imagine those fast-talkers very easily instilled false dreams in those roomy rural heads.

My own brother's head was turned by the wiles of a man who claimed he was a Boston lawyer, though his reputation was merely that of a drinker, my folks said. He quickly filled our poor Johnny full of nonsense; promising to involve him in advantageous business dealings with certain people of means. Before our eyes he was transformed, his accent, his gestures, even his clothes suddenly changed as he shape-shifted from a typical country hayseed to the sophisticated city slicker he now aspired to be. He started using alcohol and tobacco, and generally being obtuse, even with my brothers. My parents tried to talk sense into him, but he wasn't having a word of it. It was still early in the new century and he was a strong, vigorous youth setting out to prove himself. Evansville, once so subdued and pious, was changing fast, and temperance was going out of fashion.

My German forefathers had turned out to be very mighty brewers and vintners. Now there were saloons on every corner, far outnumbering the churches, with several large breweries doing roaring business, and many new temptations—the theatre, the casino, all sorts of places regular folk would never have dreamed of entering. My brother, apparently, became quite the dandy, dressing up with all the bells and whistles that befit a Bostonian of the upper echelons, and he even took to staying in fancy hotels and living the high life with his business partner during their mysterious dealings. It didn't take long for poor Johnny to burn through all his savings and get himself into serious debt. One day without warning, his fine friend simply disappeared like a puff of smoke and left him to face the consequences.

I was too young to grasp exactly what happened, but in the end my father had to go and sort out the mess for him. Money had to be found from any source possible, and there were a lot of tears and general misery about the farm—my mother even had to sell the family keepsakes left over from her dowry. When it seemed like it was all over, Johnny's hard times were only just beginning. He lost all confidence in himself and fell into a lasting depression, drinking heavily and frequenting the dregs of Evansville society. Late at night, I would hear Mama at the kitchen table, wearing out her rosary with prayers for his redemption. "Bring back my son, bring back my son," she whispered. As the eldest male, he should have been an example to his younger siblings, and his strength was vital to the running of the farm, so the entire family's future looked uncertain.

Jonathan hid himself away from us, suffering, trying to come to terms with the lessons he had to learn. We kids suffered along with him, constantly looking for the right words or for some little gesture of affection to cheer him up. Though little seemed to penetrate his dark mood we kept trying—the juiciest, reddest apple, the thickest slice of bread, the comfiest seat in the buggy were all for our older brother. It worked slowly, but every so often we would catch a glimpse of the old Johnny showing through. I recall one particularly fine day in May, out of nowhere, he burst into tears in front of myself and our brothers and made us pledge not to fall for easy talk and empty promises. I didn't really understand what he meant, of course, but I carefully stored away those words in my heart anyway, like a keepsake or a talisman to stave off misfortune. Something had changed in my family; we understood instinctively that the enchanted existence we had previously enjoyed had run its course. The spell was broken, as if the charm that had protected us had been lost. We were entering uncharted territory and would soon encounter greater trials and hardships.

Johnny didn't have the brazenness to show his face at Sunday Mass anymore, and we never sang our hymns together again. It was a small mercy that Grandpa Josef had passed away before these troubles, otherwise he would surely have blamed himself for not raising a proper, God-fearing grandson. The thought occurred to me, though, that he was somehow watching over my brother, guiding him, because I began to see little changes. Although Johnny no longer came to church, he began working just as tirelessly on the farm as Josef himself used to. Sundays, he shut himself away, staring out from his own personal labyrinth, ruminating and reflecting on what path to take next. The blood of generations of headstrong pioneers ran hot in his veins, the world of the new century was becoming ever more restless, and the desire for freedom was taking hold of him once again.

CHAPTER 5

MY BROTHERS GENERALLY CONSIDERED me quite the oddball when I was little, and of course, I was the family pet. As the youngest, I was talkative, gullible, and fell for every gag. I was always putting my foot in my mouth; though I sometimes embarrassed them, they mostly enjoyed having someone around that was so easy to make fun of and so disinclined to hold a grudge. One holiday we went for a family picnic on the grassy banks of the Wabash River. We kids all took off our clothes and charged into the river for a swim. The water was cold, still, and crystalline. For the first time, I was old enough to realize that I was seeing my brothers naked. To their hilarity, I was surprised and confused to notice that they were all made differently to me, though I had no idea what those differences might mean. I hardly thought about that kind of thing at all, not until years later, when I had a nasty experience with a boy in town. That day left its mark; I became fearful and self-conscious around men in general, highly aware of my female condition. At the same time, I was very grateful that God had placed my brothers around me to protect me and keep me safe.

There was an annual fair on the shores of the Ohio, a big event for Labor Day, or was it German Day, perhaps? Anyway, I remember the Ferris wheel, the rides, the big tent, and the cranking music box. It was very warm. I would have been about fourteen years old, I guess. I was wearing my favorite dress—white with periwinkle blue flowers on it.

Grandma had braided my hair and tied it very prettily with two blue ribbons. Since it was so hot, she'd even let me wear my ankle socks, leaving my shins bare under my smock. I remember I was sitting on a wall listening to the music, I was smiling and squinting, and soaking up the sun. I didn't notice a boy was staring at me. I had no awareness of my body yet, I was still small for my age, and I had hardly realized that I was developing, my dresses not sitting quite right on me anymore. The boy came over and asked me what my name was. He smelled bad—I wasn't one to judge, but I remember that very distinctly—perhaps it's the only detail about him that I recall with any accuracy.

He wanted to show me the workings of the Ferris wheel behind the colorful hoardings, and I followed along like a lamb. I see myself now looking back—such an innocent creature; curious, docile, eager to go and play. As soon as we were out of sight, he grabbed me by the arm, pulling me towards him like he was going to kiss me. I froze for a second, then yelled with all my might. I was no singer like my friend Amy Cox, but I was still a country girl with a good pair of lungs. My screeching startled him and he loosened his grip; that was all I needed to break free. I blundered out into the sun, still screaming like I was on fire, and my brothers heard and ran towards me. Johnny saw me first, white-faced and howling. I sobbed out my garbled story and he searched behind the hoardings and all over the fairground, determined to hunt him down, but he was long gone already.

Though nothing terrible had happened, I was shaken up for the longest time after that. There were so many feelings spinning around inside me; anger, frustration, embarrassment, and fear although I had only the vaguest concept of what might have befallen me. Most of all I felt disgust, disgust with a capital D, to the point I was almost fixated on it. The stench of his unwashed body, his dirty fingernails digging into my arm, his greasy hair, his breath when he pulled me towards him—I felt contaminated somehow. I told myself to buck up, that it was just a scare, but it was enough to put a barrier between me and strangers, especially men. I began to think that any form of femininity or sexuality was a sin, a temptation, a magnet for obscure misfortune, something that would attract a kind of danger I was not even able to put a name to. Not finding the right way to metabolize my feelings, I just closed myself off and stayed away from males, foolishly believing I might provoke them into harming me.

I didn't know about what we used to call *the birds and the bees*, but growing up on a farm I couldn't altogether hide from the facts of life. Be that as it may, I simply could not comprehend how our Heavenly Father had created such vulgar organs, "genitals"—the very word made me shiver and prickle with embarrassment—then bestowed on them the important, sacred purpose of creating life. Later Padre Peter, the kindly priest I used to confide in, told me that it all depended on the love that accompanied the act of conception. Of course, I had no idea what he was talking about. In truth we were both embarrassed and far out of our depth, just guessing at one of life's great mysteries. I only understood it many years on when, completely out of the blue, I fell madly in "love" with Frank Boever. For the first time, I began to see how there could be a connection between the feelings in my heart and the feelings in my body. It was an illuminating experience that helped me escape my suffocating safety bubble, and eventually even marry, have children, and share a life of unconditional love with my husband Don.

CHAPTER 6

HERE I AM IN my chair, still rocking almost imperceptibly back and forth, still alone. All this time just talking to myself, over the gentle whirr of the air conditioner. I thought I heard voices for a moment, but it was just the TV, I guess. Did I leave it on by mistake, or is my mind playing tricks on me? It seems no one is coming for me after all, and I'm beginning to accept the idea.

My nasty scare at the fair turned out to be just the first in a series of misfortunes. Johnny was the next source of woe: he announced to the family, with great flourish and fanfare, that he had enlisted in the army. He was going off to fight in the First World War, he said. It was the most foolish thing I'd ever heard. The conflict had been going on for a few years, but it seemed so far away from us. The United States had finally declared war on Germany some months earlier, but hardly anyone had taken any notice of the first draft, because enlistment was voluntary at the time. No one had suspected he would do such a thing; we were a family of staunch Catholics who believed in peace, in turning the other cheek and in loving our fellow man. As well as English, German was spoken in our home, being my grandparents' mother tongue, so Germany was friend not foe. We were proud of our old traditions and values, we celebrated every German day with sincere joy, just like all of the German community around us did. To me, this strange war being fought in Europe was as unreal and distant as anything in my storybooks.

We had studied the map of the world at school, learned the countries of Europe by heart, reciting the capital cities, the tallest mountains, and the longest rivers of each. I was proud of my French roots too. My father wanted me to know everything about France and he told me countless tales of his youth; the dishes his Maman prepared, the vineyards, and the terrifying old kings and queens who lived in soaring towers and castles so big that all of Saint Wendel could fit in their shadow. But there was no talk of war in my home. To me Europe was a far-off land where very important people lived; popes, teachers with funny hats and gigantic books under their arms, and there were ancient marble statues on every corner. Of course, I knew my paternal grandparents must have been over there somewhere, but it was too long ago for photographs, we had almost nothing of theirs except that battered accordion, and Papa's tales, so they were almost like fairytale characters for me. I suppose Johnny thought he was just doing what Papa and all his elders had done at his age—striking out for adventure, chasing a dream, searching for a chance to leave the past behind him, make something of himself and find glory. He never came home.

He cut a striking figure when we saw him off on the train, beaming proudly and awkwardly in his starchy uniform. That scene is etched on my heart and has never faded, even after all these decades, although I can't be sure it's all real. It's like an out of body experience; from high up in the air I observe a skinny little girl with her hair in braids, waving excitedly at her mythical older brother; suddenly, with the shriek of the train's gears and the stationmaster's whistle, he disappears in a puff of smoke—never to be seen again. A mean conjurer's trick it seems now, and a senseless one. We never really found out exactly what happened to him, just that he was gone. The loss was a massive blow to my father, who couldn't accept that the Old Country had somehow reclaimed, stolen back his eldest son. It was too cruel a twist of fate, as if a flesh tribute had been demanded, and he had paid for his own escape by sacrificing his firstborn.

Many years later, far too many, I learned that the government had opened up the National Archives so people could search for the burial places of their loved ones in Europe, tracing them back through the information they had registered on their draft cards. There were no certainties, and in the end, all I got back was a list of dozens of cemeteries where countless World War I veterans were laid to rest. Several years after that, quite out of the blue, I received a letter stating that he was believed to have been buried in the American Cemetery of Pas-de-Calais. With that in hand, my brother Eddie and his wife Kathy made the journey to France in the mid-fifties, a sad pilgrimage that at least gave them the chance to visit Papa's birthplace as well as Johnny's grave. The cemetery was almost too much for them—more than ten thousand soldiers, ten thousand identical stones, row upon row. It took hours to find the place where his name was inscribed. They returned solemn, but a little more at peace, having said a last goodbye.

After losing Jonathan, my father sunk into a lasting silence, and then subsided into a fog of depression that would never lift. He seemed to just give up on living, and he passed away two years later. I say he died of a broken heart. By now the old farm was home to just five of us—and even that meagre number was destined to fizzle out soon. We were shrinking year by year, as we sold off bits of land and most of the animals. Grandma, now the most accomplished farmer among us, was losing her sight and unsteady on her legs. We could have hired more help, I guess, but Mama was tired out and her heart wasn't in it anymore. Eddie had found work as a ranch hand and wanted to start a family. Rick had apprenticed as a mechanic; he was a free spirit and determined to work his way out of rural Indiana. He had his sights set on some big city—Chicago or Indianapolis. It seemed like yesterday we had all been playing together among the trees. Now we were losing each other.

I had been snug in my own little world, my unravelling cocoon, but I was no dummy. I could see that soon it would be just my mother and I. Mama really wanted me to make something of myself and all my book-learning, so I finally started to ponder over what my future might hold. Grudgingly, we all realized it was time to sell up and go. Mama cried long and hard over it, but she knew it was the right thing to do. So did I, but I just couldn't bear to abandon the enchanted woods of my childhood. Could we just up and leave everything like that? It felt like a betrayal, deserting our gnarled orchard, its branches arched down to the ground under the weight of the unpicked crabapples; the old barn, tiny scraps of red paint still clinging bravely to its rickety boards; and the cabin that had sheltered three generations of my family. But what else was there to do? We chose to have faith and move forward.

We knew we had made the right decision almost immediately, when a good omen came directly after the sale. Mama found a job as a companion to Mrs. Hamilton, a wealthy widow who lived in a big mansion in Evansville. She was quite a sophisticated old lady who was particular about everything, and she was often sickly and a bit of a grouch, but working for her made Mama feel useful and needed again. I was happily surprised to see my mother make her way in this new world and grow more confident every day. She and the widow formed a close bond over time, and when Mrs. Hamilton finally passed away, she left Mama a little nest egg, so that I could complete my studies with the Sisters of Providence at the prestigious Reitz Catholic High School, and even set my sights on Evansville College. Our finances were revived and those were tranquil years for me. I loved school, though it took a while to adjust from the rural education I had been given in Saint Wendel thus far.

I still recall my earliest outdoor lessons, and how we used corn kernels to form the letters of the alphabet on the ground, I was with Rick as there were only two classes; little kids just learning their letters and numbers, and big kids who could already do proper writing and arithmetic. Anyway I knew my bible well and had done plenty of reading so I wasn't too lost at Reitz. Of course the nuns were kind and helped me catch up quickly, and all the novelties of big town life were simply electrifying. It's hard to put into words just how magnificent my school was—to girl brought up in a backwoods log cabin it was just like a king's castle in one of Papa's tales from France. Built of fine Ohio brick, it was three stories high and had an arch over the entrance, as well as stone sculptures and wonderful lawns all around. Inside it held such marvels as a gymnasium, a cafeteria, a library—it even had its own candy store! It was like a special kind of heaven created just for youngsters. That's why I decided to become a schoolteacher, and though I didn't wander far in this life, at least I can say I went further with my education than anyone in my family before me, and that did us all proud.

But here I am running on, muddling up my story. I forgot to tell you about moving to Evansville. I remember the last day at the farm unwinding in slow motion, like they say it is with a car crash. Grandma had gone to her reward shortly before, and we were still grieving hard. Edward had already left us, using his share of the proceeds from the farm's sale to buy a small ranch in Kentucky. It was a world away as I saw it. I missed him sorely, but I admit I missed his wife Kathy even more than my own flesh and blood. She had always been like a big sister to me. She was a Saint Wendel girl, too, and we had been childhood playmates. I couldn't remember a time without her around, and I had never imagined her leaving, as it was rare back then for us locals to wander far from home. When I picture the day she left on the overloaded wagon, I see her thick hay-colored hair piled up on her head like always, her bangs damp with sweat, and her freckled face hectic from all the to-ing and fro-ing. I remember the forlorn feeling she left in me, like a cold pebble in my gut.

Rick soon found a job in Indianapolis and sped off to start a new life as a city dweller in his dream world, the Mecca of cars and races. That's how Mama and I wound up alone like castaways, drifting from our shipwrecked farm, across oceans of cornfields, only to wash up miraculously in Evansville, in the ample, tender embrace of the glistening Ohio River. Despite all our fears and uncertainties, we found sweet solace almost instantly in our beautiful new home. It was a comfortable, modern, and luxurious life, unlike anything we had known before. We lived in the leafy Hebron district, a short walk from the elementary school where I would later find my first teaching job. Our new house and garden were perfect for us and required no work at all compared to farm life. It was just like in the fairytale; not too big, not too small . . . just right! We put the two old rockers we had brought with us from Saint Wendel out on the front porch, and sat there on the long warm evenings, chattering away or reading at our leisure. There was a great big oak tree in the garden that gave us shade and privacy, and there were rows of holly bushes whose branches we used to decorate all the windowsills when Christmastime came around. It felt safe and welcoming, our journey's end.

CHAPTER 7

WE FOUND OURSELVES LIVING in The Roaring Twenties—exciting times
for Evansville, as the town was growing at an incredible rate. Horses and
carts were giving way to automobiles, and we would even see planes fly-
ing overhead sometimes. The First World War had suddenly made such
things not quite commonplace, but no longer a reason to stop and stare
either, there was even an air strip on the Baumgart land along Green
River road for a time, until a tornado swept it away. Trains ran night
and day, and the canals were as busy as today's highways. All sorts of
commerce prospered, oddities to my mind, such as nightclubs, a floating theatre, and even a private gun club. There was lots of construction;
foundries, sawmills, tile factories, brick makers and the like sprung up
everywhere. Poorer farmers and backwoodsmen started to leave the
land to become factory workers, ready to give up their independence
for the security of a fixed wage. Despite this, many local families still
had a little parcel of land all their own, so they could have a garden, a
vegetable patch, and some trees to love.

We dwelt in the shade of the giant oak, our sheltered island, just
mother and I. At home, the onslaught of progress couldn't touch us.
Beyond the gate, however, a new energy was coursing through Evansville, bringing opportunity, prosperity, and business. The way people
spoke to each other changed too though, as did how they shook hands
and what it meant when they looked each other in the eye. Deep down,

the newcomers and the old settlers didn't trust each other, and soon a rigid crust of hypocrisy began to form on the surface of our society. A conformism you might call it, a kind of polite respectability, a tainted air that was barely perceptible at first, but eventually clung to the fabric of our community. Mama and I were naturally cordial and neighborly with everyone, but these habits were slowly overcome by a certain awkwardness. We kept up our smiles and greetings, but beneath that was suspicion, and we kept our eyes wide open. We rarely socialized beyond those old friends from our parish that we had a true bond with. This insular approach protected us to an extent, but it also cut us off from all manner of new experiences, and that suited me just fine, or so I thought.

As time passed, I simply kept on living my drastically ordinary life. I guess underneath it all I was still somehow the same little girl I had always been. I'm not ashamed of that—it was a gift to have preserved that sweet, guileless child inside me, to still recall my secret, imaginary conversations with trees, bugs, and wildflowers. By then I was in my twenties and happily teaching at the Hebron Elementary School, in those days a lovely brick building with a pretty domed bell tower and two modern schoolrooms. Perhaps I was just younger and more energetic, but I certainly found my early teaching career an easier and more peaceful job than it later became. Over time I carved out niche for myself in Evansville, and I was mostly liked or at least respected by my pupils.

While Mama was still alive, I spent almost all my free time at home with her; sometimes we would go to a concert, but just as soon as we were able, we bought a radio. It was quite an event for us—they were still a novelty even in the late 1920s, and not many families had their very own radio at home. I absolutely adored it: getting news and music from all over the United States was an indescribable thrill, and shrank the distance between us and Rick, Eddie and Kathy—a distance that pained us more as time passed. When Rick told us he was engaged to Brenda, a girl we hadn't even met yet, it was quite a surprise. I realized I might soon have in-laws or nieces and nephews who would grow up strangers, far away from Mama and I. It's normal today, I know, but back then it was not how anyone would have wanted to live. Families stayed close and were better off for it, because that's what they were meant to do; to stay close enough to lend each other strength in the bad times and share the joy in the good.

When I wasn't glued to the radio, I was teaching, reading and studying. I dedicated many pleasant hours to perfecting my French, and giving extra tutoring to the neighborhood children. I loved poetry, and once I was even invited to a local literary circle to recite Baudelaire's *L'Albatro* in the original French. I was very flattered, flustered, and happy, just like Grandma Gretel had been when the Owens family had taken an interest in her recipes. Around town I became a recognizable character; my students would call out "Good morning, Mademoiselle," or "Hello Miss Belmont," when they saw me out and about, and indeed Miss Belmont stuck with me even decades after I had become Mrs. O'Grady. They were just little greetings like that, but they made me feel like I belonged. It must have been obvious just how much I loved my work, and of course how much I loved feeling useful. Despite that, when I was alone, I could sense that a little part of me remained numb somehow, like I was an imposter, acting out a role rather than living my life to the full. Naturally, I had feelings, but I didn't feel them all the way through, I guess I was like a leg that has fallen asleep after too much sitting still. What I really needed was to give myself a good shake, I eventually came to realize.

When I suddenly found myself alone at twenty-seven years of age, I already felt like an old maid. Even to this day, I still can't bear to talk about Mama's unexpected passing. Let me just say that she went to off heaven without a mark on her soul, and mercifully quickly. Without her though, things lost all their color for me. Suddenly I had nobody to talk to, and my own voice sounded so loud inside my head that it sometimes startled me. I rattled about the house, touching her things, trying to decide what to keep, what to put away. I didn't know what was worse—the constant reminders of her or the empty spaces. My work kept me busy during the day, but the nights were terrible. My mind tormented me. Every predictable step of my future life seemed to plod out before me interminably, right to the end, where I would die alone and no one would notice. Ironic. Unused to eating my meals and sleeping all by myself in the empty house, I would often skip supper and lie awake imagining my untimely demise—some nights I would be eaten by racoons who would break into the house through the attic, other nights I would slip and fall into the canal while out on a stroll, disappearing silently, without protest, beneath the murky water.

Life went on despite my mourning, with the same routine as always, but I stopped socializing almost entirely. I already had a vast hoard of books at home, and now I kept adding to it and adding to it, as reading became an almost addictive medication for my grief and loneliness. I would even read while I ate my frugal meals standing at the kitchen counter, so as to avoid Mama's empty kitchen chair. I was rarely truly bored—we had such exciting novels back then and I could afford to buy as many as I wanted, quite literally stockpiling Hemmingway, Fitzgerald and everything by Agatha Christie. Inevitably, the day came when my book collection grew too large for my four walls, and so I donated the better part of it to the school library. In thanks for this gesture, they put a little plaque with my name on it on a big bookshelf. I was pleased, naturally, imagining how proud Mama would have been, but deep inside, I knew most of me was still curled up fast asleep like a squirrel in winter. I had set up my routine, and busied myself with minutiae so that I didn't have to bother much with scary things like strangers or emotions or relationships, but that rigid outer shell was gradually becoming more and more suffocating.

To break up my daily monotony, I went to visit my brother Edward and his family during the summer break. Their home was bustling and chaotic, and their adorable babies, Helen and Robert, were an absolute joy to me. Surrounded by their warmth, I began to realize that I secretly desired a family of my own. It was at Eddie's home that I met Frank Boever. It was an extraordinarily fine June day, and he had been invited over for dinner. Like us, Frank came from some mix of German stock, and had been born near Evansville. He and Eddie were both mad about country music—banjos and boaters and string bands were all the rage back then, if you can imagine such a thing. We turned the radio up loud so we could hear it right out in the backyard, and we danced. Frank was a real looker, tall with blond hair and broad shoulders. When he took my hand, I felt a shiver like ice run right from his fingertips all the way down my spine. I had never felt anything like it. I knew instantly I was attracted to him. As stunned as I was, I couldn't hide it, not even from myself. I liked that man, in actual fact, my body liked him and my mind had not even been asked for its opinion. I don't know whether to blame the beer from the cooler or the heat of the day, the scent of the jasmine blooming on the trellis, or the mouth-watering meat sizzling on the grill, but it was certainly the most intoxicating experience of my long-extended girlhood.

I spent a restless night trying to comprehend my emotional turmoil. I knew I definitely had my first-ever crush on a boy—but it was difficult for me to imagine what that might mean in anything but the haziest terms, given my total lack of experience. When I finally drifted off, I dreamt that we were making love. The dream was so unexpected and embarrassing to me, the scenes so blurry and surreal, that the next time I saw Frank I was dumbstruck with shame and turned scarlet from head to toe. Who knows where I could have got such ideas from—too many novels perhaps? It couldn't have been from the movies—back in those days you would rarely see more than a kiss on the cheek on the silver screen. Anyway, my big affair with Frank ended that same day when he announced that he was moving away, and I never saw him again. That summer was the first time I ever suffered for a man: I felt lonesome, weak, and I was fretting myself nearly sick. When Eddie told me his friend had found a good job in Chicago, and I burst into tears like a little girl. My brother was sweet. As he hugged me very close, trying to squeeze some of the nonsense out of me, he asked me if it wasn't high time I did something special for myself? A trip, he suggested—or some little adventure, something new!

He was right. I had been cozying in my cocoon for far too long, smothered by the love of my family, nourished by so many happy memories; my father's admiration, my brothers' affection, Mama's constant company. I had been living suspended in time, way back before our troubles found us, before I lost Johnny and my folks, before the linger of all those loving gazes faded away from me. That coy veil that had concealed me from the advancing world was finally lifting. I had hidden at school, at work, in my scant, glancing interactions with my community, and in my occasional volunteering efforts undertaken only with Padre Peter's gentle encouragement. I had made a life impervious to passion and excitement, to electric shocks and butterflies, tears and palpitations. Meeting Frank had suddenly cracked my shell, and I was peering out at the big wide world beyond. Raw and uncertain as I felt, I had no choice but to emerge.

Here I was at twenty-seven, a strange fruit—cultured, knowledge-able, and feminine, but also timid, frumpy, and quite clueless in matters of the heart. I was not young by the standards of the day. All the girls I had been at school with were already wed, and most had at least a couple of kids, so I was seriously quite at risk of being considered a spinster. Waking up to that notion, I suddenly panicked; had I been moldering on the inside while the world around me had been gallop-ing by at breakneck speed? Naturally, I had had some suitors over the years, some perhaps would even have made good companions, but I had always kept them at arm's length. That part of my consciousness had been rudely awakened that day at the fair and then firmly locked away until the moment I felt the touch of Frank's hand. I had simply never pictured myself as a grown woman, let alone a wife, mother or grandmother. Meeting Frank transformed me into a different person overnight, a metamorphosis that was long overdue and irrevocable.

Once I had come to terms with it, I felt it was time to welcome my new status, and begin the next stage of my life with new intentions to match. I wanted to become a woman; to fall in love, to go steady, to get married, to feather a nest, to have babies. There was just one hitch in my plan—the lack of suitable candidates. On the one hand, the boys from Evansville were not quite to my taste; they were mostly factory work-ers or ranch hands, uncouth and predictable, what we used to called backwoodsmen—rednecks or hillbillies I guess people would say nowa-days. On the other hand, I wasn't nearly wealthy enough to socialize in the "better" circles in town. My level of culture intimidated most of the people I tried to ingratiate myself with. The few friendships I had were based on a certain polite distance and respectful formality: I was ac-cepted as a nice lady, skilled, educated, pleasant, and refined. That said, absolutely no one saw me as marriage material, which required a very different set of attributes.

I don't altogether regret my late start in life, sentimentally speaking. There were advantages to being quite grown-up before I finally chose a mate. As young women, we sometimes feel hurried along by our urges and impulses, which can often lead to making poor choices. Some of my friends rushed into inappropriate relationships, whether pushed by social pressure or fear of being left on the shelf, or by the ticking of their biological clocks. Luckily, I never fell for that because my family had given me a firm set of principles and indelible rules to live by. Not like my poor friend Agnes. She was such a pretty girl, but she didn't have a penny to her name, or anyone looking out for her, so she was easy pickings. She got it into her head that the son of one of the richest men in town was going to marry her. She fell pregnant, and he told her to get lost, but she must have lost her mind instead—she threw herself into the Ohio River and that was the end of her and her baby.

It was a dreadful story that blew up a storm in Evansville, and for a tiny instant it seemed like the lid would be lifted on all of our small-town bigotry, but then some other scandal came along, fresh gossip, something less distasteful to whisper about, and everything went back to normal. I often used to bring flowers from my garden for Agnes. Sprays of tiny white blossoms we called baby's breath, though I'm not sure that's their real name. I laid them on her grave for her and her little one. I don't know why but I've always thought she would have had a girl, and I called her Lia, because it sounds like a flower name, and because I needed something to call her by when I prayed for their souls. I've lived so long now, and times have changed so much, I wonder what sense that tragedy had, if any? Why did those poor, lone creatures have to die such a hard way? What happened to their souls? I still cherish them, even if no one else did.

CHAPTER 8

I'M STILL ALL ALONE here, still dead I suppose. Does this mean I'm not going to heaven? This can't be, I can't have gotten everything that wrong. Am I in Limbo? Why am I still possessed by this flow of thoughts and words? I can't stop, I'm like a radio that's been left on in an empty room.

I know what it's like to live on automatic pilot. I used to live a sort of half-life, but 1929 was the year of my awakening, my "rebirth." That was when I started living intentionally, making decisions, taking deliberate actions, and then taking responsibility for their consequences. Before that, I hadn't ever really had a sense of purpose. I was just floating along, cradled by my certainties like baby Moses in his basket. In 1929 I realized I was neither an infant nor an old maid. On the contrary, I consciously chose to believe that I was quite a fine young woman. I had charm and I was gifted with the intelligence to understand life's deeper meaning. Taking stock of my existence, I could say that my career was respectable, I earned my own money, and Mama's house was all mine now. I had a few good friends for company, and most of all I had my brothers who had helped coax me out of my cocoon. Not too bad at all!

Now it was my turn to act, so I started by forcing myself to socialize and experiment, to find out what I really liked. I began frequenting the Majestic Theater, (once a vaudeville house I would have been ashamed to be seen in), and there my love affair with cinema began. It's almost impossible to describe to one of today's youngsters what the movies were like back then, what they meant to my generation. It was like being sucked into a magic portal where anything was possible. They were such beautiful creations, and always evolving year after year. I remember the shock of the first talkies, the musicals, the excitement, the heroines. I adored Laura La Plante. When *Show Boat* came out it was as if they'd made a movie about Evansville itself. We had our own *Cotton Blossom* steamboat, even if ours was just a pleasure cruiser that skimmed the placid waters of the Ohio. I took a trip on it more than once, and it was a pleasure indeed to enjoy our beautiful river, gliding along on the old paddle steamer, watching the fashionable ladies smoothing down their bobbed hair, careful with their fine clothes and gloves on the railings, while I basked in the summer breeze, free as a bird.

I could allow myself such little whims and fancies now that I was independent, and I was finally beginning to craft my life according to my own inclinations. I have always adored being on the river, seeing the colors of the sun reflected all around me, like a giant spool of golden silk unrolling forever, pulling the sky down under the boat as it advances. Sometimes, walking along the river path, I would just stop and watch the setting sun blending into the water, the world around me turning orange then red then purple, and the shadows stretching their long cool fingers towards me. I had all the time in the world then. When no one was around and the river was still and empty, I would imagine the natives, the Delaware maybe, silently paddling their canoes downstream towards the mighty forests of Kentucky, feathers and fringes moving silently above the slate clean water. I've always been a dreamer, mostly dreaming eyes wide open, straining to catch the last gentle glimmer of twilight. Peaceful, alive, somehow part of the water, the earth and the heavens; that was how my hometown made me feel, and I loved every drop, every leaf, every blade, every miraculous whispering inch of it.

The year 1929 was my best year ever, but that October 29th would also be the beginning of decades of recession and depression all over America, the horrific stock market collapse that changed everything. Until then, the Roaring Twenties had seen the economy boom and soar to dizzying heights with an air of unconquerable euphoria. Money was everywhere, even if it was hard to see where it came from. We lived with this ephemeral sensation of abundance, of forward momentum, which turned out not to be based on a concrete reality, I suppose. What started as the most exciting and adventurous year of my life suddenly spiraled into a whirlwind of romantic chaos. Remembering Eddie's advice, I wrote to Rick. He had been married to Brenda for a few years by then, and asked him if they would have me to stay for a while. They lived in Indianapolis, and I wanted to spend some time with them and finally get to know my little nephew Bernie before he got too big to be spoiled rotten by his auntie.

I also wanted to explore the city as it was fast becoming a very fashionable place—there was talk of skyscrapers, highways, even a brand new autodrome. I left in July, suitably attired in a green dress with white polka dots and matching white hat, gloves, shoes. It was natural back then that I would wear my Sunday best for the train journey. Ready for adventure, I remember I had a slender notebook with me so that I could jot down my impressions of the trip, but I don't recall if I ever wrote anything in it, I think I just stared out the window. It was only the second time in my life that I had ventured beyond Evansville unaccompanied. I was starved of novel experiences, new colors, new flavors, new acquaintances, anything to whet my appetite. I was curious to visit places I'd never seen before, but more than anything else, I intended to uproot myself from the familiar comfort of my daily routine. I'd sworn I wouldn't let myself slide back into my comforting provincial normalcy—its subtle embrace was soft and deadly like the insidious mudflats of the Wabash River. I was on the search for nothing less than a meaningful new existence.

Indianapolis, it turned out, was neither so very far nor so very different from Evansville, but to me it was a vast metropolis of first times and exotic wonders. Every day I would paste a new memory over an old one, a new image of youthful, happy Lucy over the frumpy old one. That timid, bookish school marm had been left behind, and the new me was a woman of the world, a girl about town, even. I smile now to think how naïve I was: today we can voyage to outer space, get on a plane and hop across the globe, the idea of "going away" is harder and harder to understand. Does it really mean anything anymore? In my day, two hundred miles seemed like another world. My train arrived late in the evening, but I found Rick waiting for me. I was all a-chatter from nerves and excitement on the way to his house, and my brother was bursting with news too. Brenda and the baby were already fast asleep, but we talked well into the night about his new family and his wild life of automobiles and city folk.

Rick was absolutely mad about his job and about Indianapolis, where the trend for motor racing was really at its height. It seemed like everyone on every street corner was talking about race cars, and the new obsession was speed. The city itself was growing faster and faster, its broad avenues now boasting fancy museums, elegant memorials, the huge round plaza, the obelisk, they were even building a cenotaph. It hardly seemed real to me that I could actually visit these foreign exotic things, once just words and pictures in an encyclopedia. I could walk up to an obelisk and touch it! My brother, it transpired, had become not just a passionate citizen of the new age, but also a very talented mechanic, and had a good, steady job in the Ford factory. His lovely wife, Brenda, whose luscious auburn mane betrayed her Irish heritage, worked in retail. She was a shop assistant in a gigantic new department store and looked as glamorous as a movie star. I was delighted to see how their purposeful lives were structured around jobs they loved.

My little nephew was sheer perfection—a bubbly, chubby, love bug. Though barely toddling, he always eager for a trip to the ice-cream parlor or the park. In those carefree weeks I often took him to the leafy local park to play on the grass, and we were never in a hurry to leave the swings or the sand pit. I was amazed to see that many of the kids in the playground were accompanied by paid nannies, not mothers or grandmas. It took me a moment to figure out that working mothers were already almost common in Indianapolis, though still rare as hens' teeth in Evansville, where only the richest families had nannies. I suppose in Indianapolis folks were more sophisticated—even the city center was incredibly futuristic; I remember feeling like I was on another planet when I visited the brand-new plaza, so clean and perfect with its graceful, soaring fountains spraying cool mist everywhere. Then there was the day I encountered my first actual skyscraper. I was so struck by it that in spite of my usual shyness I walked right to the front entrance as if I owned the place! I took off my glove and touched the cold polished stone of the doorway as I craned my neck up, but it was so tall I couldn't see where the building stopped. It was impossibly big and modern, and more frighteningly, overbearingly handsome than anything I had ever laid eyes on.

Brenda taught me all about big city chic. We went to the best stores and she talked me into loosening my purse strings. Her eye for fashion was undeniable, so I put my clueless self in her capable hands. She helped me overcome my modesty and taught me how to show myself off a little. No detail was left to chance; we even went to her fancy hairdresser where I got the short haircut that was all the rage, with a little fringe that flicked out just like the actress Claudette Colbert. I felt like a starlet. I don't think I ever loved another haircut so much. Then came a generous application of makeup, my first real face paint. Thank heavens that the Sisters of Providence couldn't see me now, I thought—such vanity! Rick barely recognized me when we got home. The Saint Wendel spinster had become a sophisticated city girl, and it was all thanks to his gorgeous wife. Brenda made such a fuss of me; I had never had so many compliments in my life. She wanted to do something special to celebrate my transformation, and Rick had the idea that we should all go to the racetrack. He was often at the speedway and relished any excuse to be around cars, of course, so that was how I went to my very first day at the races, and how my life got completely turned upside down.

CHAPTER 9

My name is Lucy Belmont and I am telling this story as best I can, although I'm making a mess of it, and it seems even Death himself isn't listening!

Where was I? Oh yes, that summer of 1929, and all dressed up like a turkey on Thanksgiving, I was brought to see a race at the famous Indianapolis Motor Speedway. There were thousands and thousands of people, and an incredible buzz of excitement about the place, but it was so overcrowded that I couldn't make head or tail of it. It was quite late in the afternoon but the sun was still searing, the noise was deafening, and the air smelt like gasoline and overcooked hot dogs. Our seats were quite high up in the stands, and the cars lining up to race looked like children's toys to me. I was simply bewildered, as I sang along with the band playing "On the Banks of the Wabash." After a while, I became quite uncomfortable in all the make-up and finery. Perching on the hard seats, watching those tiny vehicles flash by in the distance, I began to regret my drastic haircut as the sun scorched the back of my newly exposed neck—but what was there to do?

Brenda was thrilled and agitated; she'd spotted a VIP client of hers in the good seats and was doing all she could to get herself noticed. Rick had disappeared somewhere to mingle with his acquaintances and talk motors or some such. Sweltering, I made my way through the stands to the restroom and did my best to refresh myself without ruining Brenda's masterpiece. When I came back, Rick was chatting with what I can only describe as a tall, dark, handsome stranger. He was startlingly attractive, with an athletic build, jet black hair, and a square jaw. "Here's the brains of the family," Rick exclaimed as I approached. I blushed crimson, of course, but it must have given me an attractive glow because the stranger looked into my eyes and smiled. He had a devastating, Gary Cooper smile. Really, I'm not exaggerating, I wish you could have seen him back then, he was a knockout. "I can't say if she's the smartest lady here, but she sure is the prettiest," he said, grinning. I might as well have been struck by lightning. Suddenly I was breathless, and so stunned I don't remember another thing about that whole day!

It turned out that the stranger was Don, a friend of Rick's and an expert mechanic like him, as well as a racecar driver. The next day was Sunday, and he was invited over for a cookout. Of course, my brother and Brenda were conspiring on my behalf, and I was as transparent as a sheet of cellophane when it came to feelings. Now, I don't want you to think I was just some boy-mad ninny who fell for every man she set eyes on; he really was something special. As the men lit the grill, Brenda made potato salad and I fussed terribly over little Bernie to hide my embarrassment. I felt so silly and awkward, and I had no appetite at all, so I just pushed my food around my plate and kept my eyes lowered. I knew if I even glanced sideways at our guest, I would surely turn bright red again. Eventually the heat of the evening relaxed my jitters enough so I was able to speak. Don was the center of my attention, naturally, and I was surprised to find myself asking him question after question. With him, my usual shyness around men gradually evaporated. By nightfall I found that we spoke easily, our words intertwining almost of their own accord. Our separateness disappeared as our stories slowly knotted together, and they've remained that way forever.

I simply *had* to know everything about him. With my relentless prodding he eventually unfurled his whole life story, spreading it out before us like a picnic blanket. Don's father was called Leonard O'Grady. He was Irish American and had all the typical Gaelic traits—a handsome, good-natured charmer who was afraid of nothing when he had a drink taken, though he was actually born and raised in Brooklyn, New York. His people were farmers back in the Old Country who had come to America with nothing, fleeing the famine,

Don said. Though Leonard never been to Ireland, he knew all the old songs and sayings, and loved reciting them to his boys as if they were nursery rhymes; "You have to eat seven bags of dirt if you want to go to heaven" was one of his favorite dinnertime phrases, and Don joked it was his father's shy way of saying Grace. Life moved faster in those difficult times, and barely turned eighteen, he met and married a lovely Italian girl called Teresa, although everyone called her Resy. She had come to the New World when she was just a child, all the way from the village of San Marco dei Cavoti near Benevento in Southern Italy. She was anything but typical of a woman of her day, I discovered. She went to her reward too soon, but in her short life she managed to provide a moral compass for her two boys, Frankie and Don, and her influence was so strong that both of them decided to leave the crime ridden neighborhood they were born into and instead train for solid professions. My brother-in-law Frankie, as gentle as he was talented, opened a barbershop and led a serene and admirable life. I didn't get to see him very often—we really only met at the usual family weddings and funerals. I regret that now, because he was a good person and you could tell even without knowing him well, because his grandkids are all educated and have good jobs. One of them even went into politics . . . maybe one day he'll be in the position to make a real difference in this world.

All I really know about Mama Resy is that she was the proud daughter of Angelo Ferraro and Concetta Costanzo. The Ferraro family were wealthy landowners in Benevento, and even had some distant claim to nobility, apparently. Angelo had benefited from a good education by the standards of his day, and he had been a Justice of the Peace. He drilled the importance of hard work into his children and grandchildren, insisting they must each have a skill or a trade. Working with your hands, he said, was the surest and best way to earn respect and reputation. He had a sort of motto that he repeated often: learn a good trade and you'll be a rich man wherever you go in this world. It was as if those words were tattooed on Don's brain, he lived and breathed them; know your trade, work with skill, be tenacious, fight to be the best at what you do—and those were the core values he really wanted to imprint on our children too, when they came along.

The Ferraro name was well known, and all of Mama Resy's siblings became prominent folk. They opened food stores, worked hard, and made good money; even today their great grandchildren still have shares in a big supermarket chain that they founded. One of the youngest is a professor and travels all around the world giving conferences on supply chains and some such. I asked Don why Grandpa Ferraro had decided to leave a privileged position in his native Italy and try his luck in America: Don said that he'd wanted to escape the burden of being the firstborn son in such a famous family of land barons. They were all wrapped up in their ancient rules and ways of doing things, while he'd wanted to start his own dynasty—and in the end he succeeded quite brilliantly. When he died, a huge crowd attended his burial, and his wisdom, which Resy had inherited, was spoken of by many. His death was a great loss for the Italian community at that time. Sadly, I don't know much about *Nonna* Concetta; she died young from tuberculosis, they say she was very sweet-natured.

Thinking back on how strong the family ties were in those times, in my family and in Don's, I realize now just how necessary a strong family nucleus is. It's the foundation, the very bedrock of a well-structured individual and a balanced society. The knowledge handed down from generation to generation is the lymph that nourishes the processes of social evolution in our world, and this should be a source of great joy to us. I have always been convinced that if you possess knowledge, you live more deeply, with more humility, more awareness and empathy. That's why I'm proud that I never tried to hide my humanity from other people: as a daughter, a sister, then as a teacher, a wife, and a mother. I was simply as a creature that grew, grew up, grew old, and absorbed all sorts of experiences along the way. I lived, sometimes surviving, sometimes thriving, through the entire twentieth century. Periodically, as time passed, I tried to understand what was changing around me and to react to those changes without being swept away by fads or fashions. I was always tethered to, and by, my deepest beliefs and moral principles. Sometimes I ask myself, wanting to be neither trite, nor merciless nor unpardoning, how will the coming generations manage to structure their lives? People split up, they remarry, yet they don't realize that their own children, in turn, won't easily be able to build their lives in the proper way if they don't have strong foundations to sustain them as they try to make it through to adulthood. To our children, we are like the legs of their chairs, we can't just move around willy nilly and expect them not to slide about.

It takes a strong and flexible backbone to come through life's storms and chaos. The rough times cannot be avoided. They are the mysterious tool life uses to put us to the test, to make us overcome our resistance to change and face our fears. They make us understand gratitude and appreciate the true depth and richness of our existences. They are the harsh pruning that makes our fruits hardier, makes us grow stronger and better than we ever imagined we could. How can today's children stand and face life with only quicksand underfoot? And how will our future history read if no traces of fixed values remain? What have we set in stone for them now? Unquestionably it will be a lot harder for them to stay faithful, not only to themselves, but also to whatever external moral duty they undertake. So many people choose to just give up when things get rocky nowadays; they don't have the patience or the desire to face those inner challenges. I wish I could see into the future; maybe from where I am now, I'll be able to see more clearly.

When I entered into Don's inner world and became part of his story and his family's story, I began to know his dreams. At that time Don worked for Ford Detroit, and he had a famous ear for engines. People said he was able to listen to them like he was listening to music, and diagnose what was wrong. Though he dropped out before his diploma, he had had some technical schooling and was trying his best to work his way up in his trade, following his grandfather's mantra. His consuming passion for automobiles often drew him to the track at Indianapolis, where he tested and drove racecars. It was a dangerous job and sadly, a horrific accident would cost him the amputation of a leg some years later. I know I've said it before, but my Don was a real looker—he could have been a big Hollywood star, I promise. His looks lasted well into the years, his lashes were dark like his thick wavy hair, which only started thinning when he was far too old for vanity. He had beautiful strong hands too, though often etched with grease. Even after his accident, he was the most handsome man in the world to me.

His smile was irresistible, as was his easy charm; his way with the ladies came from both his Irish and his Italian heritage. He would always sing for me—*Fenesta Ca Lucive*, an old song from Naples; for years I was convinced that "Lucive" was a way of saying Lucy . . . then I found out it meant something like glowing or illuminated, it was a song about a window that glowed with light. But whatever it meant, it didn't matter, when he sang that melody for me my heart would just melt in my chest. Don thought I was a little ingenuous, of course, but I'm happy to say I always remained a romantic, and a dreamer. I was always a naive country girl at heart . . . even when I realized the love of my life had destined me to live out my days at a busy crossroads, alongside a gas pump. If I hadn't been raised so strong and patient, I might have given up right then, and I would have missed out on so much, perhaps even missed my destiny altogether. Luckily though my roots were deep, unshakable, and I trusted myself and the person I had chosen to build a future with.

When the Green River Road began to grow northwards, Don saw his chance to make his dream come true and bought a fine piece of land, where we would eventually build our forever home, as well as our neighborhood's very first gas station. In the early days, our place was a corner of heaven. We dug a big round flowerbed, where I planted my beloved irises. They bloomed every May without fail, in a magical ring of fragrant happiness. There were huge trees all around our house that protected it, not just from the heat but also from the stinging odor of gasoline next door. Don called it "the smell of money, the smell of work." I hated it, it polluted my little paradise, but I understood: it was his job, one of the few things he was still able to do well, after the accident.

Somehow, I could never totally forget about that smell of gas, it never grew easier to accept. All the same, I loved my husband instinctively, with every cell in my body. I still dream of him. Now I'm leaving this old carcass behind, with all its aches and woes, I wonder—will I touch him again? Will my soul touch his, or will we be young again, or maybe even like children? If this is death, it's not a bad feeling, there's nothing bothering me at all, it just feels awfully muffled, muted, and blurry. It would be marvelous if he were here with me in this quiet place. I imagine he would feel just like I do right now; finally free of pain, with no weight on his shoulders, his body made whole again. I almost sense him nearby, like if I just stretch far enough, perhaps I could brush his sleeve with my fingertips. My mind slows when I think of him. It is such a relief from the chatter that's streaming through my head, I can finally think straight! But I've run far too far ahead . . . I must put my tale in proper order for the last time.

CHAPTER 10

MY NAME IS LUCY, I'm ninety-seven years old, and here I am chattering away to myself, just as I have for the past decade at least. Is there really any difference between being alive and being dead?

Something is bleaching away my memories. I feel light as a sparrow now. I know I have to go quickly otherwise I'll lose everything—but how do I know this? Is the Mystery coming for me? Where was I? Don? Have I even told you how Don proposed? It's funny now, in retrospect. Rick and Brenda realized immediately that I was completely lovestruck though I thought I had been very discreet. I knew what I felt was much more than a crush, not that soppy feeling I had had for Frank—this was something utterly new. It was a feeling of belonging with another person, like a home-coming almost, as if I had been missing him all along. I think Don actually felt the same thing, in his own way. Despite having a reputation as a bit of a Don Juan, he telephoned me as soon as he got back home to Detroit and even invited me to spend Thanksgiving with him although it was months and months away. Back home in Evansville, everything suddenly felt new to me. I was infused with an energy unlike anything I had ever felt before, and everyone could tell that I was a different person from the one who had left.

After the holidays I got back into a routine; school, cinema, walks or little trips on my bicycle, my books, and of course my radio. I listened to just about everything I could and compared the news with what I read in the *Evansville Courier*. It was the radio that informed me of the financial catastrophe that had shattered the stock market without warning. It was October 1929, and the Wall Street crash was sending shockwaves all over the world. Don and I had been writing to each other regularly during the fall. In our own words, our feelings for each other timidly came out, and we shared all the ups and downs of our daily lives. In November, however, I received a letter that quite frankly stated his intent: "My darling Lucy, things are going from bad to worse here and I fear my job won't last much longer. I don't know what to do, I dearly want to marry you and build a life together, but I cannot ask you to leave your beloved home to live with me in this grey city where I have no hope for the future. If you want me for your husband, find me work in Evansville and I will come immediately."

I was quite dumbfounded by this blunt "proposal," so I called Rick for advice. He confirmed that the situation was indeed becoming desperate there. Luckily, he felt his job was safe, but Brenda didn't know how much longer the department store would remain open. Then I turned to Edward, who told me things were not so bad in Kentucky and that we would all manage one way or another. He reminded me that our grandparents had been pioneers who could handle anything God sent their way. Now it was our time to face the unknown, and the spirit of America was calling us to have faith in our land of opportunities. Eddie made sure I didn't lose hope, reminding me that I had a safe job, a house all of my own in Hebron, and two brothers ready to help. With those level-headed words, suddenly I could see my future taking shape, with Don, in my beloved Evansville.

We were married just before Christmas, right at the peak of the crash that would become the Great Depression. Though it plagued the next decade of American life, we didn't care, we were young and madly in love, and that was all that mattered. Padre Peter married us, in front of God and a small gathering of close friends and family. That evening was the first time Don sang *Fenesta Ca Lucive* to me. We hadn't known each other for long, and had rarely been alone together, so the wedding night was not easy for me. Mostly I remember that I was petrified, and so terribly ashamed of my own awkwardness. My mind and body were in turmoil, my thoughts flashing uncontrollably from fear and embarrassment to the commotion I felt whenever Don smiled or when our eyes met. With him I felt so different from before, although our strongest affinity lay in our thoughts, our dreams, our goals in life, more than in something sensual. My husband was a virile man; solid, real—he enjoyed making love. Sometimes I regret that I wasn't a better lover for him. He seemed to understand me, though, disarming me with a few honest words: "I prefer you this way; I went out with a lot of women, but afterwards I didn't have anything left to say to them. You're different." His words were always simple, but I knew they came from his heart, because I felt them warm my bones and soothe my mind the way lies never do. I wish I had been more of a lover and not just a wife, but it wasn't in me, I guess. I do know I couldn't have loved any man on earth more faithfully or more completely.

We found our perfect rhythm when we were older, when Don's virility was waning and we could focus more on what we had in common; spirituality, morals, our own shared inner world. Don was very religious, but he could never find a match for his kind of faith inside the church walls. He didn't trust priests in general, but then again, he found it easy to put himself directly in contact with God, so he had little need of them. He was intense in his habits, respected the principles of our faith, and had an enormous dose of Christian charity in him. Many Evansville folk still fondly remember him for his many little kindnesses. He loved working with youngsters and did more than his fair share of volunteering—coaching, the scouts, mentoring the boys he gave summer jobs to in his garage, no doubt sharing Mama Resy's wisdom with them. Years ago, he joined the local Rotary Club, back when it was an easy-going social club not the posh affair it became later on. Don was never one for formalities, he never saw himself as a real entrepreneur or anything like that, even when he was awarded an honorary citizenship of Evansville in recognition of all his work for local youths. The boys he coached adored him. I just wish he could have had the same sort of relationship with his own son as time went on.

I suppose these ironies are part of life, and we just have to take the good with the bad, the ups with the downs, but sometimes it is very hard indeed. Even the happy days after our wedding were soon followed some awful events that I still can't make sense of even now. The worst one of all was the tragic death of my dear friend Isabel Soanes, in childbirth. It was a test that almost proved too much for her poor husband

Carlos. I'm sorry to give you just these snapshots of life here and there, and expect you to make a straight tale of it, but how else can I untangle it now? I bring it up because Carlos had an automobile repair shop, and that terrible loss brought an unexpected opportunity Don's way. Carlos was distraught and decided to move back to his hometown, Austin, where his folks could help him with the tiny newborn. He asked us if Don would like to take over his business, and suddenly my husband found a perfect way to set up on his own in Evansville and really become part of the fabric of the town, despite the fact that the country was still mired in the Great Depression.

Thinking back, I'm truly amazed at how our lives can often be governed so casually by an extraordinary mystery like death. It is wrong to be afraid of death, because it is an expression of God's will, like everything else. And God's love for us is so immense that it fills every hole and balances every scale in the end, if we can just hold on long enough. You'll think I say that lightly, but believe me, I have had my share of loss and then some. I've just lived long enough to know that if you have faith, sooner or later, something good eventually comes along and makes you glad you didn't give up. In Austin, Carlos met and married Mary, who loved his little one like her own. A few years later, they had a baby girl they called Isabel, and that name, so well loved, became a living part of their family again.

Don was thrilled to have a new start, and he quickly made a name for himself locally as a talented and honest mechanic as well as dealing in spare parts. Before long he was making a good living, and soon we had a shiny new Chevrolet in the driveway. I used to feel positively giddy when I heard the wheels on the gravel, and I'd rush to the door to welcome him home. He always cut a fine figure, handsome and simple, and all his little ways of doing things were beautiful, too, in their own right—like how he would never enter the house before taking off his hat, or how the first thing he did on arriving and the last before leaving was to kiss his proud wife. He was thoughtful in ways I never imagined, nor indeed expected, from a husband; he was careful around the house because he knew how much effort I put into keeping it nice, and somehow, he would always put just the right amount of milk in my tea or cream in my coffee. We had our petty quarrels, of course, mostly about the kids when they came along, but we never stayed angry for long and we learned to forgive quickly. Even after a big blow up, sometimes all it would take was a certain look or a half-smile to make peace. As often as not, I could just stretch out my hand and brush his arm, and we'd start giggling like teenagers.

In those days our love came in the form of empathy. We practiced understanding each other, willing ourselves to accept our differences and be thankful for what we had. Needless to say, people didn't live together before getting wed back then, and I suppose you'll laugh at us now, but my husband and I had twin beds from the first day our marriage to the last. It was considered the modern, heathy thing to do in the late twenties when we set up home together, and was certainly the norm until well into the fifties, at least. As a matter of fact, I don't think I ever saw a blatant display of a double bed in a magazine or a store window until Eisenhower's days, or perhaps even Kennedy's. Anyway, Don and I didn't worry over things, we just let them come naturally, so every little detail we discovered about each other was fascinating, and the early years flew by in a happy blur. Our firstborn, Gregory, arrived in 1932. Two years later Teresa came along. How can I tell you what it felt like to finally have children of my own . . . and with the man I loved more than anything else on earth? It was a miracle, a physical manifestation of what we felt in our hearts. They made us more selfless and caring, and gave us a common goal. Suddenly every choice we made was for the good of the family. They were Don's greatest gift to me, and mine to him. Our children were the pearls that our love and faith created, and the source of my greatest joy and pain.

CHAPTER 11

THOSE WERE DIFFERENT TIMES, but all in all our little family's early days were happy ones, and the long-awaited end of World War II brought boom times back to the USA. Suddenly everything was as upbeat and optimistic as the Boogie Woogie dancing that was sweeping the nation. It was around then that Don first got the idea of buying that plot of land for us, something that would provide some security for when we were older, and when he found that spot along Green River Road, way out in the countryside, he knew it was the one for us. He'd heard this was where a new part of the city was planned, and where Evansville's very own Speedrome was going to be built so drivers wouldn't have to race their cars on the horse-racing track anymore. It was the perfect place for Don's dream; a home for us and a business all his own—a gas station. He knew all about the developments on the way because before his accident he had competed in a lot of races. He even won some important ones around the Tri-State area and was still on the board of the organizing committee.

It was during a test run before a race that he lost his leg. When he wasn't at his shop, Don drove anything he could get his hands on; motorbikes, midgets, stock cars, whatever came his way as long as he could move fast and make money. On occasion, a driver of his level could win five hundred dollars in a single day of racing and, given that he could build and repair his own vehicle his costs were low, so it was lucrative and enticing. I suppose I was just blinded by love, or perhaps I lacked the imagination to think much about the danger. All the wives and the owners used to sit together during the races, some of us would bring potluck—it was like an impromptu party. I consider it a great mercy that I wasn't at the track the day of his accident. I'm told he lost control of the car, perhaps due to an oil slick, and slammed sideways into the guardrail, destroying his right leg and fracturing his shoulder and pelvis. The accident was horrendous and it took every ounce of strength that he possessed not to give up as he languished month after month in a hospital bed. A friend of his took over the shop so we could manage, money-wise, but his new life as a cripple was almost too bitter a pill for him to swallow. It changed him, adding a wary, acidic taint to his personality. Although he survived and kept on going, things never went back to "normal" and I knew he made the effort more for the kids and I than for himself.

As soon as he could work again, he tried starting back as a racecar mechanic, but his mobility was so limited that it became too much for him. For a while he tried his hand at selling cars too, but he was born to fix things, not to make deals. In any case, his dream slowly cemented into reality along Green River Road. When he finally hit on the idea of opening a gas station, the local customers flocked to him, because he was always happy to advise on their car troubles while he was filling the tank. I think what counted most for him was that he could finally be the one to provide a home for his family, instead of living in what we all still thought of as Mama's place. We decided to put the house in Hebron up for sale, that way I could add some money to the project, and still keep something aside for our children's college funds and our retirement. I was amazed by what a good price it got; unbeknownst to me our quaint neighborhood, with its neat rows of houses and their well-kept gardens and borders, had become quite sought-after over the years. I had never really considered selling until then, and I thought I would be distraught packing everything up for the move. In actual fact, I felt surprisingly blessed and energized instead.

Love is a mysterious thing, and it comes at you from all angles, when least you expect it. Mama had bought that house for us with the money from the farm, and using that inheritance made me feel like she and Papa were still embracing and protecting me from up above. Truly, I could feel their arms around me—I was still their precious little girl, even though I was a wife and mother myself now. Love like that never really goes away, it just changes form. It was the final dose of nourishment that I could take from the wild land that had once been ours, that had fed and watered and shaped us with its goodness. I said a long farewell to the Hebron community, to the oak tree, to the holly bushes, the fireplace where we'd hung our children's first Christmas stockings, and all the wonderful memories. We had two children now, and perhaps more would come, so we needed more space, and it was time to move on to something new with the strength of my forebearers behind me. It was an exhilarating prospect, at least to begin with.

Our plot was on the corner of two main routes, and there we built our very own house from scratch at the intersection of Green River and Morgan Avenue. It was much farther away from my job at the Hebron Elementary School, but I was in seventh heaven. Green River in those days was just a country road that led out into endless expanses of cornfields and wilderness, so I felt like I was back in my childhood, in Saint Wendel. Don and I had spent months planning every tiny detail of our new home and the life we envisioned for our family. We had so much land Don almost didn't know where to begin, but I knew exactly what I wanted; dozens and dozens of fruit trees. Another thing I had always longed for was a great big covered patio, so I could stay outdoors gardening much of the year, whatever the weather. Out back we put the garage where Don set up his workshop, and then there was an old barn, which we fixed up with new clapboards and painted Venetian red so it looked just like all good storybook barns should. I didn't get much of a chance to enjoy it though, as it instantly became the exclusive domain of our children.

It wasn't all perfect right away, little Resy missed being close to her school and her friends and the genteel charms of the Hebron community, but soon she got her first bicycle and felt the thrill of freedom on our almost deserted stretch of country road, just orchards and cornfields as far as the eye could see. Naturally, that bucolic tranquility didn't last many years, all too soon Green River became a hub of suburban development, and we were awoken from our rural reveries by a whole new town sprouting up right on our doorstep. It was sad, but it also brought business and gave us true financial security at long last. The house wasn't some gigantic luxury mansion like the one our new neighbors Frank and Kitty Madison built, it didn't have a tennis court or a swimming pool, but it was perfect for us. Don and I had gone over our plans again and again, so it was as special and unique as the four of us were. We had put something different in it for each of us. Night after night, just as soon as the kids were in bed, we would roll out our blueprints and spend hours fantasizing about our future together, forever, just like a fairytale. And it was perfect home for many years as we grew into this new Evansville home.

My oversized bookshelves flanking the fireplace were the focal point of the living-room; Greg's piano was in a corner a little out of the way, so that his playing was pleasant company, but never invasive; Resy's room had a lovely view of the orchard and a big canopy bed fit for princess. I simply adored the bright new kitchen with its Formica countertops, all new appliances, and windows facing east and south. We had four bedrooms, a bathroom with a great big tub upstairs and another downstairs—we were so spoiled. One of the bedrooms was carefully decorated for guests. While I painted the walls a delicate primrose shade, I imagined my nieces and nephews sleeping there. Yes, they were a bit too grown up to fuss over by then, but I still wanted to pamper them and keep them close. In the basement, we had a laundry room with an automatic washing machine and a built-in wringer. Just think what it meant to me. When I was a little girl, a backyard well and an outhouse were the height of luxury, no one I knew had indoor plumbing! To this day, I can still see Grandma Gretel tackling with the wooden mangle we had in the yard behind the cabin—it was a fierce beast that only she could wrestle into submission.

When everything was all done—or as done as it would ever be—we threw a big house-warming party: my brothers and their families came as well as friends and neighbors. That year we had an enormous Christmas tree so tall it touched the ceiling—not one of those horrible plastic things they have today, a real one that scented the whole house with fresh pine for weeks. The kids and I made most of the decorations by hand; heaps of painted pinecones, strings of popcorn, little parcels made with scraps of wrapping paper and bits of ribbon. It was so beautiful I almost cried when the time came to take it down, so Don took a picture of it for me and put it in a pretty frame. I still love to look at it even now. It was the best of times, back when Christmas was still Christmas, not "the holidays."

CHAPTER 12

WHERE WAS I? My name is Lucy Belmont, but once upon a time I was also Mrs. O'Grady, and Mom to two treasured children—Gregory and Teresa, or Resy as we always called her. Our firstborn, Greg, was robust and willful but also a very sweet child. He loved to play with his toy cars, making them race over the floorboards. He was barely more than a toddler when Don built him a tin car with pedals, all of his own. It was his greatest treasure—it must still be out in the barn somewhere even now. I couldn't have asked for a better son—he was imaginative, bright, and a patient older brother. You know, he always did well at school too, and he applied himself in every subject, though he truly excelled in art and in music. As doting new parents, we used to dream of our Greg growing up to be an engineer and designing cars or trains or even airplanes one day. Instead, over time, he seemed to lose interest in motors and decided to do something totally different with his life.

At about sixteen years of age, he fell in love with Jazz, and all the wild music that was coming out in the euphoric post-war years, which eventually developed into the beatnik craze. He studied guitar and piano, and finally chose to pursue a career as a music conductor. I like to think that, in his own way, he followed in his father's footsteps after all, though he used his keen ear for music, not motorcars. I was delighted by his choice of profession as I knew this was a new milestone for our family, and a wonderful opportunity for Greg. He had chosen a limitless path where he would never stop learning and growing, both intellectually and culturally. Music was not just a talent of his, it was the love of his life, he once told me, and it was where he excelled and felt his happiest. Although he never became famous, he had a fair amount of success touring with his music. He even made some recordings that sold quite well, and in later life, he earned himself a stable job teaching music at the University of Chicago. He truly loved being a teacher, maybe he got that from me. His students loved him too, and he used to get so many thank you letters from them, some still sent him Christmas cards, photos and news about what they were up to for years after they had graduated.

Virtually everybody in Evansville knew Greg through his music, and he was on stage during many special moments for our local community gatherings. Whenever a ribbon was cut or a speech was given, there he'd be with the orchestra, and we were always in the crowd cheering. One of the proudest days of our lives was the inauguration of Washington Square in 1963. It was a new town plaza that was the centerpiece of a plan to give Evansville a real heart again, a place where people could just meet up for a chat and spend time together without the traffic whizzing by constantly. To me it was a symbol of our desire to keep our community spirit alive despite the rampant expansion going on in every direction imaginable. Greg's music was marvelous, so powerful and thrilling, capturing the jubilant atmosphere perfectly. That very day I saw Don finally realize just what a special man our baby boy had grown up to be, both professionally and personally. He was moved to tears, though he tried to hide it, and I pretended not to notice. We were both so proud of him we could barely speak.

All the same, as the years wore on, I often got to wondering why Greg never did follow his father into the automobile industry. Where did the intense love he once had for motors disappear to? Can love like that just go away, or did something happen to ruin it for him? After Don's terrible accident, which led to the amputation of one of his legs, his personality changed dramatically, and he became impatient, even intolerant. At the time Greg was still just a little boy; needy, immature, maybe it didn't take much for him to withdraw from Don, to close himself off emotionally. Perhaps he distanced himself so as not to be overpowered by all that pain and negativity. Did Greg lose his first love to his father's anguish? Or was it my fault—did I fail to nurture and protect him, or to instill him with enough strength of his own? Did I truly understand or even know my son? Perhaps it all worked out for the best, as it was destined to all along. My Greg had more than just a phenomenal ear, he had a fine mind and great artistic sensitivity. Not aggressive by nature, perhaps he would have been wrong for the competitive, violent, random world of motorsports and racing. Looking in from the outside, at least, it certainly seemed to me that he found true joy in his chosen work. When he was conducting, he seemed enraptured, wholly absorbed by the interwoven harmony of notes and sensations that music is made from. That was the only glimpse of his inner world that he allowed us. His private life, revealed years later, was a great surprise to me.

What can I tell you about my Teresa? Everyone agreed that Resy was a very lovely little girl. I often used to look at her sweet smiling face when I was tucking her into bed at night and think, how can she be mine? Like all the best fairytale princesses, she was beautiful on the outside, but her true beauty came from within. Indeed, she was the distillation, the very essence of all the finest gifts and virtues of our two families put together: kind and wise like Mama Resy, dark eyed with long thick lashes like her Daddy, a cloud of wayward hazel hair like her Grandpa Bernard, gentle and good like my own dear mother. She even had the voice of an angel when she sang in church, but growing up she never wanted to cultivate it. "One musician in the family is more than enough," she used to say sagely. I think she wanted to leave the limelight for Greg, she was always considerate of her big brother that way. She was the best of all worlds, although sometimes I was a tiny bit envious, wishing she were a little less like the others and more like me. I'd never have admitted it back then, but I was such a goose, the typical adoring mother, and I wanted her all to myself.

We didn't look alike at all, but we did have plenty in common. We played together all the time—dress-up was her favorite game, and it always began the same way: she would hop up onto the velvet-cushioned stool at my vanity table and demand a visit to the "beauty parlor." She was obsessed with anything she found in my vanity drawer—my tortoiseshell hair combs, a silver-backed bristle brush that was a wedding gift from Brenda, my collection of Valentine's day cards from Don, he never forgot a single one. Her makeover was always the same; first came eyeshadow, then a dab of perfume, then the clip-on earrings that made her yelp, which she insisted on wearing nonetheless, then an old lilac-colored shawl with a very long fringe draped around her and pinned together with my big sparkly broach. Finally she would slide her tiny feet into a pair of high-heels and parade around on the bedroom carpet, stumbling and giggling non-stop, pretending she was all grown up.

When she did get a little older, she actually turned out to be a real homebody, just like me. One thing we both loved to do on rainy days was sit in front of the fire and rummage through boxes of old photos. Naturally, they were mostly black and white, but Don always used a professional camera for taking shots at the Speedrome, so we had some Kodachrome pictures too, and even some precious recordings of the children's recitals, or Easter egg hunts, or their usual Christmas morning shenanigans. We never got tired of those memories. Resy also shared my passion for reading and we would spend whole afternoons at the library, or treasure-hunting in my bookshelves. Pride and Prejudice, Wuthering Heights, Great Expectations; she was a hopeless romantic and read more for sheer pleasure, for the thrill of words, rather than for learning or edification per se. We never tired of chatting about our favorite books and authors, which ones had most surprised or delighted us, the few we disliked or couldn't figure out; they became like a group of friends we loved to spend time with. The thought never crossed my mind that someday she would be gone.

I was besotted with her, but if it was at all possible, her father doted on her even more than I did. She was the apple of his eye, Daddy's best girl, and for him she could do no wrong. He once had a necklace made for her with the word Teresa on a gold chain, after her namesake grandma Resy, and he even brought her with him to the Speedrome a few times, given that Greg often didn't seem keen to go. Resy tried her best to take an interest in the world of automobiles, just to make Don happy, but it was not her thing at all. Her sunny disposition made her a pleasure to be around, she was good at games and sports of every kind, so she always had plenty of friends to play with. She was a true daughter of this River City, so she loved the Ohio and was a natural at swimming, diving, even water-skiing. Whenever she was asked what she wanted to be when she grew up, she would come up with something new; a tightrope walker, a pirate, a magician, a giraffe, an archaeologist.

To my relief, after high school, she chose a different path entirely. I was on cloud nine when she told me she wanted to become an elementary school teacher. Children adored her and she adored them. I could see her walking the halls of the Hebron school just as I had. She easily earned a place at Saint Mary-of-the-Woods College in Indiana—a gracious all-girl institution, just perfect for our little princess. The day she graduated was one best days of our lives. As I watched her walk on stage, I felt my heart swell with pride, so much so I thought it would burst right out of my chest. Then it happened. That same day, still beaming in her cap and gown, Resy introduced us to Bill Coleman, a dashing young Australian she had met at a campus social event. My swollen heart burst and I collapsed like an empty coat falling from its peg.

Finding the air suddenly absent from my lungs, I was quite light-headed as we all shook hands and made the usual polite noises. Ah! The irony, the cruelty, the horror of getting what you wish for. My girl had turned out just like her own silly romantic mother after all. I could see it in every fiber of her being, she was head over heels in love with this foreigner—and lost to me forever. My own first meeting with Don, that lightning strike, passed before my eyes. I realized there and then that Resy would abandon Evansville and take off with her new beau—the sun and moon and all the stars to her now, but a poisoned spindle to me. What a vicious punishment life had doled out to me so unexpectedly for such a minor transgression as envy, I thought. Talking it over with you, I see now just how far off track I was back then—when had I recast one of the seven deadly sins as a *minor* transgression? That was certainly not how I had been brought up to think, and I don't imagine now that I have the wisdom to rewrite the Bible for the better.

As I feared, just a few weeks later Bill went to Don and asked for her hand in marriage. The year was 1958, The Platters were singing "Smoke Gets In Your Eyes," and our sweet baby Resy, now Mrs. Coleman, was leaving for Sydney. Seeing the newlyweds off at the airport, I felt a tidal wave of emotion sweeping over me. As Resy disappeared beyond the departure gate, only Don's arm kept me upright. It was all over before I knew it, a cascade of shattering losses. Their engagement party, the preparations, choosing the dress, pinning on her veil, cutting the cake, even the wedding vows had been a blur to me, a vale of tears. Don and I hadn't really had any time or money for a proper wedding, and had to make do with something simple, so my baby girl's should have been a magical experience. Lord knows how many times I'd dreamt of her wedding day as I watched her grow up—her snow-white communion dress, her prim confirmation suit, her lavender prom dress with its enormous poodle-skirt. How could she be leaving me? I hid my turmoil, chastised myself for my selfishness and smiled through the big day as well as I could, but it hurt so dreadfully.

Nothing was worse than actually watching her walk away from us that day at the airport. It reminded me of Johnny, his train disappearing into the distance. Sometimes foresight is a gift, sometimes a curse; there have been moments in my life, few and far between, where I have regretted my God-given intelligence. This was one of those moments. I knew with absolute and irrational certainty that I had lost her forever, and with her my vision of the future. Don and I would miss the most important moments of her life, and never grow old with her and her children nearby. It was a hopeless situation. I eventually resigned myself to her absence, her rejection as I perceived it to be then; it was her path and her choice so I had to accept it after all, but the pain of it never dulled. I see now that I let my resentment get the better of me, and that was the true source of my pain, not my poor Resy.

CHAPTER 13

THIS PLACE I'M IN right now has no regret, no pain, no thirst, and no hunger. It's neither too hot nor too cold, it's just right, and here I am suddenly feeling quite snug and quite smug even, just like Goldilocks did before the bears came home. Back then though, with Resy gone, our dream home on Green River suddenly felt cold and echoey. Greg always seemed to be away somewhere, touring with his music, and I'm sure he didn't want to be rattling around the house without his kid sister for company. Anyhow, I found my days were emptying away without purpose. I just didn't seem to want to do anything except brood over my daughter's departure. Slowly, however, thanks to Don's patience and insistence, I began to come out of my fog. I realized we had a new job to do; my husband and I had to relearn how to live together—just the two of us, alone again. We set to work on the problem with the same tenacity and diligence we applied to everything else and in the end, we hit on a fabulous idea. In a determined effort to recapture the brave the spirit of our youth, we decided to plan a big trip to Europe.

Our grand tour was designed as an homage to our roots. Neither of us had ever left the United States, and we had long dreamed of visiting all the fine places our parents and grandparents had told us of, although we knew that World War II had since destroyed much of their beauty. Our little family had passed through the last war relatively unscathed; Don was already too old to enlist when it broke out, and Greg was too young, but many of our friends and neighbors had suffered the pain of seeing their sons go off to fight, never to return. It made no sense at all to me that the USA had gone to war in Europe for a second time, especially when most Americans had never been anywhere near the old continent. All the same, the radio kept hammering on that we had to make the sacrifice, to be a beacon of hope, to defend liberty and the pursuit of happiness—the American dream no less. Apparently, it was our duty now to help mold Europeans into something more like us, so they, too, could benefit from our fabled lifestyle and our economic stability. Such airs and illusions we all had, and how quickly it all unraveled.

At the time though, so much of what was ordinary to us was still unheard of in many parts of the world. Evansville had so many factories that there were all sorts of inventions being manufactured daily on our doorstep. I remember shortly after Mama and I came to Hebron, the old Hercules buggy factory was torn down and replaced by a huge plant making refrigerators and ice machines. Thousands and thousands of people worked in just that one factory, Servel it was called. It ran like a miniature city onto itself, and because of it, Evansville even became known as the refrigerator capital of the world. You have to remember that this was a time when a typical European household would have had a larder at most. Don and I also purchased our very first air-conditioning unit from there, a wondrous new machine they had created, and it worked like a dream in Evansville's unforgiving summer months.

Of course Evansville was always a place of invention, because its German founders were born builders and makers, it was just in their blood. Helen once told me that the real inventors of air conditioning were a German Christian sect called the Harmonists, who had created their own way of heating and cooling their houses perhaps as early as the 18th century. Certainly, when they settled in New Harmony and built their lovely town, they were already masters of many ingenious techniques. The walls of their homes had a series of inlets and tunnels inside them to circulate air and regulate the temperature, and then there was something they deliciously called "Dutch biscuits," though in Helen's tale they turned out just to be cleverly placed wooden wedges wrapped in mud and straw, for insulation.

During the Second World War, the Servel plant began producing the wings for Thunderbolt aircraft, but when it was all over, it quietly returned to making peacetime appliances. The wheels of industry were always turning. Things slowly got back to normal, and my beloved Evansville blossomed again, as did the rest of the nation. I was well past middle-age by then, but I think the fifties and early sixties were some of the best years for my hometown. Everything seemed to be ripe with wealth and good fortune. Lots of big companies had opened up and demand for labor was at an all-time high. Hardly anyone was out of a job or down on their luck, and everyone had cash to spend, at least on pay day. Like the rest of Indiana, people were for the most part conservative, quiet and law-abiding. Racial discrimination still influenced social norms, and even from my sheltered perspective, I clearly remember the bad old days when schools, public transport and even cemeteries and residential neighborhoods were segregated by color and by religion. In spite of these problems, in Evansville there was so much industry and prosperity that almost everybody could find work and build a life, so we didn't suffer quite as much unrest and violence as bigger cities.

Most of the townsfolk were still of German or European origins, many not even American by birth, and not mother-tongue English speakers either. Then there was a large African American community with its own neighborhoods, schools and churches, then a smaller Jewish population. Everyone I knew had a religion of one sort or another, mostly Catholic, but there were also Lutherans, Protestants, Episcopalians, all sorts, but all believers in something. There were even some Harmonists in town, who taught living-room seminars on meditation. I was always curious about other faiths, and it was easy back then to see the common ground between them all. I once went to a talk given by the principal of the Evansville African American School and he was a very distinct citizen and a graduate of Dartmouth University, who it turned out would soon have an important political career ahead of him.

Then, of course, there was a constant influx of poor, dreadfully undernourished immigrants from England, Ireland, Italy, Spain, Poland and all over. The American dream shone before their eyes, as it did on the silver screen, and floods of hopefuls were once again making their way to the promised land, the land of opportunity, just as my people had before them. The great state of Indiana offered work for all, and we Hoosiers became almost popular—it felt like it was our moment. Evansville had a fine reputation as a prosperous, spacious, verdant place where a hard worker could get ahead, and attracted families from all over, especially England. Hordes of newcomers came to us in waves, found happiness and put down roots, though of course the biggest draws were still the major cities like Indianapolis, Ohio, or indeed Chicago, which was finally free of vice and making leaps and bounds towards becoming one of the most beautiful and modern places in the United States.

We prospered too, in those fortuitous years. The gas station was going great, and alongside it we had built a little convenience store selling bits and pieces, firewood, newspapers and whatnot. Busying himself with our affairs, Don had been able to pull himself out of the depression his accident had catapulted him into. With the extra income coming in I eventually gave up teaching. Nearing sixty, I was tired out—older but perhaps not wiser—and somehow the students seemed to get harder to handle with every passing year. I decided to dedicate more time to myself at long last. When I left, the Hebron School held a retirement party for me, and many of my old students who still lived in town were invited. Lots of them worked in the local factories. Observing what were once "my" little boys and girls, who I had helped to grow and prepare for life, I had mixed feelings indeed.

On the one hand, I was genuinely happy to see them again after so long, the tenderness I'd had for them still alive and well inside me. On the other hand, it pained me to see what many of them had grown into. They seemed so clumsily molded, so tragically well adapted to their modest daily lives. Where had their spark gone? Some very bright children had been turned into some very dull grown-ups. Where once were cheeky grins, twinkling eyes, fast tongues and strong agile bodies that never sat still, now were slouched shoulders, balding pates, worry lines—but they were still just youngsters, or middle aged at most! They should have been full of vim and vigor. What had I spent all that time away from my own two babies for? Had I really put so much effort and passion into growing these precious little saplings just to feed them into the mulcher of progress? Factory fodder they were mostly; button pushers, switch throwers and lever pullers whose daily grind had turned their minds and bodies to mush in a way that honest farmwork or ranching never did. They looked atrophied, wilted, as if they barely moved all day, yet they bore clear signs of stress, and seemed exhausted.

Was this the modern way—did regular life and a regular job now flatten an individual into a shadow? People had done hard labor in my day too, and worse still often began working as children, but somehow, I had never seen a cigar roller or a telegram operator or a saddler or a boatman similarly drained of vitality. How had this happened? A world of senseless contrasts spun before me—how could a whole generation be overfed yet undernourished, overtired yet under-stimulated, adrift in life, yet always busy, no plans beyond the weekend, yet fearful of whatever new scourge the future might bring. A lucky handful had managed to escape the herd and set up on their own, a few others had gone into sales, or nursing, and there were several engineers. The University of Evansville had always had an outstanding faculty of engineering what with all the manufacturing going on in the area. I guess seeing some white collars among them soothed my vanity somewhat and made my long service as a teacher seem more worthwhile, but all in all I was in a mire of mixed emotions.

Should I just say it outright? I had expected better for all of them, taken it for granted I suppose. I know you'll think I'm a snob, and me just a farmer's daughter putting on airs, but that's not what I mean at all. I had thought their dreams would come have true by now, or at the very least that they would still be chasing the tail of those visions. Where were all my little ballerinas, and astronauts, and veterinarians, and quarterbacks, and arctic explorers, and presidents? Where was their American dream? Did they remember any of it? It was all still right there in my memory, clear as day; their vibrant, frenetic drawings, how they played make believe with such fervent conviction and delight, how they could instantly transform a cardboard box into a rocket or a castle or an island. I could still feel the full blasting force of their sheer will-power, how they couldn't wait to grow up so they could do anything and fix everything and go everywhere, and all at once. I had thought they'd have the world at their feet, born into such a rich and fertile land—instead they were mired down, floundering in uncertain terrain—where had their dreams gone? I just stood there disoriented, caught in a sort of time warp, and no doubt the very picture of a befuddled old goat long overdue for retirement, when in actual fact I would probably have still been a hair shy of my sixtieth birthday. My mind was clear as bell, but it just couldn't make sense of what it was seeing.

It was then that Samuel Smith saved me. He made his way through the crowd like a knight of old, and swept me into a massive bearhug, almost knocking me over in the process. "Hello, teacher," he exclaimed and presented me with a beautiful bouquet of flowers and a handwritten thank you card. As I read the words, I realized I could still recognize his wobbly calligraphy, I could feel my hand on his, molding his fingers around his chewed-up nub of a pencil, scratching out his first smudgy letters. Time crinkled up like a sheet of scrap paper. We were back in class again—and I was so happy to see that little boy. I laughed, I sobbed, tears rolling down my face for all to see. I didn't mind one bit; I was just so overcome by wave upon wave of memories. Samuel had been a really hard case. He came from a rough family and the whole town knew his mother drank herself silly to survive the beatings his father gave her whenever he would show up. His older brothers had left home and enlisted as soon as they were old enough to escape, and both had died in the war. At home it was just Samuel, his mom and a toddler.

Now I won't lie to you, he was no genius in class, but he was a good boy, a hard worker and, all things considered, a lot smarter than he gave himself credit for. I did all I could to help him believe in himself, and to support his studies; he would often come and talk to me after class when he had troubles, and I tried to guide him as best I could, even after he moved on to high school. One day he called by to asked me about university scholarships. I could see the hope in his eyes, the hope of a real future one day, of escaping to a kinder fate than that which had befallen his brothers. Hand on heart, I had to tell him that with his grades it was not on the cards, but I did advise him to open his own business, a little shop or something where he could make the best of his excellent people skills and his enterprising nature. We stayed in touch: he found job in a seed nursery and worked his way up to having his own florist, all the while studying horticulture at night school. Once he started making money, he was able to help out his mother and his little brother, who he as good as raised.

So, in the end, both siblings were able to rise above a harsh beginning, and create a new life with dignity and meaning. Today he has a chain of stores all over Indiana and is a successful businessman. Whatever I did to help that happen was the highpoint of my teaching career, and it made my shortcomings and errors seem less terrible. I know you might say it's not the teachers' fault if their students' dreams come true, but I think that every teacher, indeed every capable adult, has a precise duty to do their best for every little soul they encounter and help them make their way in this world. If parents can't manage it someone else must; relatives, neighbors, bus drivers, coaches, preachers, shopkeepers, anyone at all who has the opportunity. We are all in this together and a word of encouragement costs nothing. Every growing spirit needs inspiration, motivation, someone to believe in them and give them a gentle or even a hard push in the right direction now and then. We shouldn't just stand back politely and watch all their hope, all their sparkle and brilliance wear away.

After the party, although I'd officially retired from teaching, I realized I wasn't quite ready to box myself up in mothballs. I decided to volunteer at the school a couple of days a week, to stay busy and maintain some sort of a daily routine. There was always such a lot to do, like secretarial work, keeping track of supplies, organizing afterschool activities, or being a reading buddy. Even though I was tired out, I still needed to feel socially useful. I couldn't just go cold turkey from my teaching routine—I needed a reason to get up in the morning and get out of the house, plus I missed the hustle and bustle, the kids, and the eternal challenge of trying to channel all their chaotic creativity into a day's work and play. It's only when you quit working that you realize what it gives to you. As my career gradually faded into memory, that tiredness I was always grumbling about shuffled towards a form of mild regret, and then finally mellowed to bittersweet, then sweet memories. I had loved all those kids and I had loved my job; it was that simple once I laid aside my disgruntlement and vanity.

As time passed, my character continued to ripen and my body endured all sorts of weathering without too much fuss and bother. I was no different than the heavy autumn fruits I encountered as I strolled in the shade of my orchard each afternoon, indulging in my own private form of walking meditation. I seem to remember reading a lovely phrase somewhere that went like this: if youth is the prettiest flower, then old age is the sweetest fruit. To become a teacher had been my childhood dream after all, how many people can say that they made their dream come true? A part of me had always secretly feared that my dream was too modest, too humble, that I hadn't really pushed myself enough. But thanks to my career, that wonderful role of teacher, I had been able to keep on developing culturally and spiritually year after year, maturing my mind and spirit, making my family proud, honoring my father's memory. I had had precious afternoons and long summer holidays with my own two pearls, my children. Aging made petty fears and anguish melt into a wonderfully soothing nothingness. Now I have finally gained sufficient perspective to understand what discernment really means; no more senseless, abstract guilt, no relentless negative self-judgement. What counted for me was simply this—that I had done my honest best, and that my loved ones would have been proud of me, and that's really all there is, don't you think?

CHAPTER 14

THOUGH IT WAS A surprise to me, after retiring I slowly came to realize that my relationships with my students had made me more compassionate. I had acquired patience through my work, and that patience seeded true kindness in me, and a touch of bravery that brought me out of my shell around others. My job had made me feel that there was a space in the world specifically meant for me to fill. I was nobody special, but I had been able guide and support all those children towards the future. I'll never feel that I did enough, but I hope I managed to show each of them that they were unique and gifted in my eyes. Those kids helped me to understand people in general better, too. Day after day they taught me how to listen more carefully and hear the truth between words. That's why, even as the decades wore on, I always managed to make sense of the changing times and maintain a feeling of connectedness to the world around me—because they had planted a little of their youth and imagination deep inside me.

As well as my armchair traveling, in my silver years began to dedicate more time to art. I loved leafing through the big books of paintings I found at the library: there weren't so many artbooks about back then, not like those gorgeous, glossy, colorful ones you find in fancy bookstores nowadays. If I could snap my fingers right now and travel anywhere, I would transport myself to Barnes & Noble in Evansville, so I could just sit and be surrounded by those gigantic books on the old masters and the Impressionists. Of course, I really haven't been in any kind of store for several years; I wonder if they're different now. Looking at all those pictures made me feel like an explorer, like I was peeking through a magic window into another dimension. They made my mind come alive, and now it seems so obvious that such a thing as art therapy should exist, although I'd never heard of it then. I also wish I'd at least tried painting a picture, the thought did strike me several times, but I never seemed to get around to it. I regret that laziness now, as I'm sure I wasted quite a few hours in front of the television when I could have been teaching myself to paint or draw. My cat Chou Chou was one of the most elegant and least mobile creatures I've ever encountered, and would have made the perfect sitter for a portrait. I'd be glad of the company of that soft, silent gaze right now.

One thing I did tackle properly, once I had settled into my retirement, was some serious reading. I began challenging myself, as I was determined to keep my mind active. I took an interest in science and even cosmology for a while, but it was heavy going. Soon enough, I found my way back to softer topics like philosophy and psychology, then sociology and history. I was shocked by just how much I didn't know about any number of things really. Did I tell you that little old Evansville had two enormous public libraries even back in those days? And both more beautiful than someone visiting a town our size would have any reason to expect? Resy and I loved the Willard library, with its gorgeous Gothic architecture and its resident lady ghost, but Greg always favored the Vanderburgh library. It was an Art Deco wonder, and had a listening library that was a world onto itself, a precious resource for him. Evansville has been known for many funny things over the years, from barbeque to refrigerators to oil even, but I like to think it of it as the library capital of the USA. All human knowledge can be found in our libraries, free of charge and immersed in loveliness.

Am I drifting again in my story? Meandering? Memories coming and going, tempting me into deeper waters, as irresistible as the ebb and flow of the tides. Random thoughts. Incomplete. A riotous swarm of swallows ricocheting in the darkening sky of my mind. I know I must keep telling my tale, but is anyone listening? I have no anchor now. As a retiree, as I think I had started to say, I had my volunteering to pin my daily routine around. I slowly weened myself off my dependence on the school, but I still needed something to get out of bed for, otherwise how does one go on? I have always found it vital to live according to some kind of set rhythm. As it is with a tune, so it is with life, it must be played out in order, not too rigid but not too loose, and it must be done with solid awareness. Each of us must create the precise harmonic composition will become the symphony of our lives. And like music, it's not easy, it takes practice. Part of my practice involved spending more and more time in the parish, and I signed up for two literary circles, one for literature and one for psychology. The latter turned out to be my salvation in the cruel times that were soon to come.

I was reasonably content to have stepped back from working, but I didn't feel crumbly and old inside yet, some days I actually had more energy than ever. I had certainly never been so well rested in my whole life, so I began to hunt for some novelty to perk things up—a touch of the exotic, something to give a little flair to my character perhaps. I wanted to stand out a little, to be more eclectic, continental, anti-conformist, rive-gauche even. I felt it was high time for another makeover, but I didn't quite know how to go about it by myself. From Reader's Digest, of all places, I got the idea of trying out some new habits by inserting quirky little rituals into my daily routine to spice it up. During the summer evenings I'd wait for twilight, *l'heure bleue* as Papa used to call it, then I'd light some scented candles on the patio table and settle into my recliner in time to see the first stars pop out. Sometimes I'd sit out there for hours, long after the lanterns burnt out and dusk turned to darkness, just breathing, reminiscing, and stargazing. The stars were wonderful in those days, countless swirls of twinkling dots; white, pale blue, purple, green, red. And the sky! Oh the sky was a marvel, baby blue by day and inky, obsidian, infinite by night. The Milky Way passed right over our house, making my garden hideaway seem part of the universe. Can you imagine some children have never gotten to see such a sight? There should be a law against stealing away the night sky.

When I was feeling ambitious, I'd bring an atlas and a torch out into the garden, and study the sky chart, memorizing as many constellations as I could before the task overwhelmed me. I suppose I succeeded in cultivating a touch of eccentricity. It was well before the hippy craze began, so this wasn't the kind of thing everybody did. I finally had a dash of bohemian flavor in my life. Tucked away in my padded sun-lounger, behind the big thick evergreens that hid the house from the road, I furtively eavesdropped on the sounds of the night. Sometimes I would hear young lovers whispering to each other, sneaking out late to go parking outside town, but as time went by the streetlights and the increasing traffic on Green River Road drowned out all those little trysts and secrets, and slowly the habit faded away. Eventually, I put my lanterns and recliner away in the barn with the kids' old toys and drew the bolt, feeling I was locking away a rebellious youth I'd never lived, a distant summer season that smelt of suntan lotion, mildewed cushions, and the late-blooming wildflower meadows of my imaginary Bohemia.

Don used to say I was a hopeless romantic. He never shared in my nocturnal extravagances—early to bed, early to rise, he said—but he did sometimes ask me what it felt like, lying out there in the small hours. "It's a whole other world," I'd reply, because it wasn't something easy to put into words. It is impossible to look up at the stars on a black, moonless night without relishing that humbling feeling of decompression they give you. The sheer, unfathomable size of our awesome universe, spread out over our heads, and the crazy fact that we are part of it . . . it simply puts every other thing into perspective. Even our biggest problems shrink by comparison. It should be everybody's unalienable birthright to look up at the stars on a clear dark night and find relief. It would have done Don good, a little star-gazing, and I had always hoped he would catch the bug for one of my interests as he grew older. Art, geography, astronomy—anything vaguely cultural would have done me—but it wasn't to be. If you want to live peaceably as a couple, you really do have to take the time to find out what your other half can give you, and what they can't, because you cannot get out of them what they just don't have to give in the first place.

I could have insisted, dragging him about to galleries or poetry recitals, to my book club meetings, he would have capitulated I'm sure, but he would also have quietly detested every moment of it. He had his own interests. When he grew to old and crotchety for coaching kids, he began to take more of an interest in his photography, though mostly he snapped cars and scenes of races that I didn't quite know how to appreciate. I'm glad I accepted him the way he was instead of trying to change him, the same exact way I'm glad he didn't oblige me to spend all my weekends at the Speedrome. This was something I had to figure out for myself over the years, especially when divorce became the new normal in our society. As time went on it seemed it was all the rage, and everyone who was anyone was getting a divorce or three—Bette Davis, Marilyn Monroe, Liz Taylor—it was everywhere. Even in our small circle of acquaintances there was one family that had a tense, disharmonious existence, though no one would ever admit it out loud. It was simply taboo. Everything was somehow obscured by a demure veil of willful blindness.

The first divorces I remember hearing about were seen as a challenge to the status quo of traditional conformism: it certainly was quite scandalous, but in those rare cases it seemed like the decisions could be considered justified. The real problem only reared its ugly head when divorce became a trend, a fashion to follow, even something to boast about. It was like a diabolical machine that grew bigger and stronger every minute, grinding up marriages at the first sign of trouble, stopping couples from ever really getting to know each other deep down, from confronting their reciprocal differences. Neither husband nor wife had to grow up anymore, there was no longer any reason to learn to deal with relationship issues, you could just give up. Multiple divorces became "a thing" as people simply charged ahead as always, making the same mistakes with new people, time and time again. Today the stories I hear, about what our society has been reduced to, they genuinely scare me: the degeneration, the corruption of a sound basic concept has spawned situations of an unspeakable moral horror. Worst of all, those men and women who were never forced to mature past a certain idealistic, perhaps adolescent, emotional state, in turn raised kids who were denied the privilege of having fully adult parents. Children raised by children, growing up without grown-ups—a kind of Peter Pan or Lord of the Flies. I can't bring myself to talk about the babies involved; it hurts to think how much suffering has been generated, how much long-term damage done, I'm just sad, and that's all I can say about it.

CHAPTER 15

DON AND I HAD our own problems a very long while back, so I'm not just some old bat blabbering away in her rocking chair with no idea what goes on out there in the real world. I may be deceased, but I still know what kind of society we're living in, let me tell you. One dark day, smack in the middle of our married life, an ill wind brought a certain young woman named Flora to Evansville. I don't know if it was fate or just bad luck, it certainly wasn't her kind of town. Whatever the reason for her arrival, she was a rotten apple, a floozy on the lookout for some silly man to mooch off, maybe even a husband to pay her bills and keep her in finery. How did I know this? Well, when any male specimen whatsoever was about, she was suddenly all curves and smiles and fluttering eyelashes. She must have seen Don at the gas station one day, when he was looking particularly dashing, and decided that he would suit her needs just fine.

I realized something was up when Don suddenly started wearing cologne to work. Then he started keeping irregular hours and acting shifty, which was very unlike him. Our town has its gossips, just like any other, and I came to know that he had been out with Flora several times in secret. I was mortified, disgusted, it was an affront to my dignity as a woman, and foolish, indecent carry-on for folks our age. Infantile, selfish, embarrassing . . . and Don didn't even have the guts to confess! What was he thinking? That we would just carry on like normal? Did he imagine that I was cut out for a ménage à trois with some trollop? Now I wasn't delusional: although I was still slender, careful with my appearance, and not unattractive for my age, I certainly couldn't compete with this fleshy, flirtatious Jezebel barely in her thirties. It hit me hard, feelings of shame and rejection dragged me down. As the weeks passed, I sank deeper into myself, not wanting to see anyone. I cried long, bitter, stinging tears. We started fighting—daily.

Late one evening, distraught, I reached the conclusion that it would have been better all round just to let him go and start a new life with his fancy woman, maybe it was the only thing that could boost his ego enough to finally get him over the amputation. I had had a secret of my own for many years: I dreamed of exploring the Gulf of Mexico. A proper journey, I decided, was the perfect excuse to get away from the mess at home and clear my mind. I told Don that things weren't working right between us anymore, and now that our kids were grown it was time for me to take a trip alone. I didn't tell him where I was going. I didn't know how he would react—and I was almost shocked when it turned out he was furious. We had such a vicious fight that even several days afterwards I still couldn't believe how much anger there was between us, how much rage. But the fight didn't change my mind, I was leaving despite the threats Don made, and the next day I went to the travel agency to plan my trip—my escape from it all.

It was May, and in the garden the iris flowers were blooming, making their magic circle of vibrant color and heavenly scent. I was in too dark a mood to enjoy it, and so mad that Dan had stolen even that little joy from me. My bags were packed, Mexico awaited. Then the phone rang. It was my brother Rick: his wife Brenda, after many years struggling against cancer, had just passed away. I dropped everything and rushed to Indianapolis to be near him and my nephew Bernard. Don arrived a day later, though barely a word had passed between us before I left. It didn't take long for the keenness of Rick's pain to bring us back to ourselves. It laid bare the true value of what we were—husband and wife, and what the destruction of such a bond really implied. We realized the value of our covenant, our love, and when we got back home to Evansville, Don stopped wearing cologne. Flora replaced him with a younger man whom she married soon after, but it didn't last and before the year was out, she was gone for good, swept out of town on her broomstick, I like to think.

The shock of losing Brenda helped us reset our emotions and heal our relationship. Finally, we were able to talk about our married life openly, what it meant to us, how important it was to stay together, not throw everything away over such idiocy. For the first time we gave some serious thought to the significance of what we had been through so far and even to how we wanted to prepare for our old age. With the passing of time, we still had a chance to grow, and this was an opportunity for truly improving our characters at long last. We came to understand that it was our duty to lay aside our vanities, obstinance and pettiness and accept that we had aged, and would continue to, and eventually die because that was God's plan for all of us. No amount of foolishness would change or delay that fact. It was also our duty to provide strong roots for our children, just as our parents had done for us. They had never let their difficulties weigh too heavily on our shoulders. Greg and Resy were making their way in a challenging world, and traditional values were going out the window at an alarming rate. Sooner or later, they would come up against their own disappointments and losses. Don and I would have to reinforce and sustain them by being a good example for them to follow, and the stability of our life together was essential to the success of that mission.

My faith shone a new light on this realization—it was a clear choice—I understood that going forward I would always fight for my marriage; it was the most meaningful experience of my life, and I could glean wisdom and knowledge within the confines of that bond that lay nowhere else. A few months later, Don came home with two tickets for San Francisco. I saw the Pacific Coast for the first time. Being together was magical, so incredible that we promised each other that we would immediately plan another big trip somewhere exciting. It was a wonderful holiday, we felt the breath of our youth in us and, from then on, we decided not to live passively, as if we were pensioners anymore: our age was a wonderful thing, still rich in new joys to discover each day. Together.

CHAPTER 16

MY NAME IS LUCY Belmont. Can anyone hear what I'm saying?

It's lonely here, just like when Resy left for Australia. I often used to find myself wandering into her bedroom, just to sit in her chair or stare at her things. To cheer myself up I bought a big new atlas and an even bigger map of the world to put up on the corkboard in her room. I stuck white pins in all the places I'd been to and blue ones in all the places my heart was set on visiting. That's how I found out that, despite all my reading and fantasizing, I had seen far too little firsthand. I had plenty of ideas about where I wanted to go. Greg was a constant inspiration—he always sent me postcards when he was away on tour; they were little gems to me and I stored them all away for safekeeping in a pretty box. Is that true? Why did I keep them out of sight? Not on the fridge beside Bernie's? Perhaps I knew my dreams of traveling the globe did not tempt Don at all. He had a terrible time getting around with his leg, and any long journey was far more of a pain than a pleasure. Nowadays there are prosthetic robotic limbs, and I hear there are amputees who are running marathons, but back then there was nothing so fancy. Or perhaps that's just another excuse, a way not to admit that thinking of Greg gave me a funny pain in my heart sometimes.

My brother Edward knew we were having difficulty adjusting to our empty nest, so he often sent his daughter Helen to stay with us. She was a kind and gentle spirit, not at all interested in matrimony, and a bit of a dreamer, just like I had been as a girl. It was such a joy to spend the afternoons with her, shopping downtown, strolling by the river, having a bite to eat. By then Evansville center had been completely transformed. Our once rural Green River had become fashionable and was packed full of diners, restaurants, and up-market boutiques, as well as lots of places for youngsters to entertain themselves. Consequentially, Helen and her younger brother Robert were more than happy to spend some time there with their aunt and uncle when they could. For Don and I, it was like turning back the clock and having our family together again. We took part in their lives with a strong and sincere sentiment, almost like a second set of parents.

Helen was young woman of course, yet she reminded me so much of Grandma Gretel, because she had that same sensitive, devout nature. For a while I thought she had the vocation for a religious life, and I do believe she would have entered a convent if she hadn't become part of the spiritual community over in New Harmony. She was fascinated by psychology and spiritualism, and was always reading up on all sorts of modern things as well; self-improvement, motivation, mantras. She was the one who pushed me to keep a diary, which turned out to be some of the best advice I've ever been given. That diary became my confidant, my friend, my comfort in my later years, and helped me maintain an open heart and mind, no matter what life threw at me. When my darling Don died, Helen came to stay for a spell "to keep each other company," she said—but she was really teaching me how to live without him. I guess she would have been forty-something then, but she was already wise far beyond her years.

Greg was in Australia with Resy, who had been very ill, and he was with her and her boys in her final weeks. My nephew Bernie stayed close to me while I was mourning and did his best to take my mind off things with endless stories of his trips around the world. He had practiced medicine in some of the poorest countries, on four continents, so listening to him I could make believe I had indeed adventured around the globe just like I'd always dreamed of. The biggest journey of my life was the one I took so many years earlier, in 1959, with Don—our long-anticipated trip to Europe. I had prepared like crazy, devouring everything I could find at the library on Paris, Monaco, Venice, Rome, Naples. I wanted to be sure we didn't miss a thing. We decided to start our grand tour from London, to see all the famous sights, and from there we could easily visit Ireland or cross the Channel to Calais and reach Avion, the village where my Papa was born. That was perhaps the biggest surprise, even shock, of the trip—there really were actual mountains, terrils they called them, built by the miners from all the slack they dug out of the ground. They looked almost like pyramids, four hundred and fifty feet high, towering over the quaint abodes of the natives! I had never imagined his funny, fireside tales as a cold reality. It was a brutal example of why he had left his home and family, why he had had to escape, and why America had truly been his land of the free, and indeed a dream home for all those brave spirits who strove for a better, fairer chance at life.

What bitter, tormented earth my father had been seeded in, and what clean, nourishing soil he had found to plant his own children in. I had never doubted his love for me, but this place made his ambition and his sacrifice for us seem infinitely greater. I cried more tears for him there perhaps even than at his graveside, so many lifetimes before. Later we visited the places where his parents and some of his relatives were laid to rest, sadly we had never met but I said a prayer for them in French, and introduced myself and Don to them, and told them that they were missed and remembered. We also managed to locate what is thought to be Johnny's grave, almost lost in sea of other veterans, almost indistinguishable, so indistinct that I wished we could have taken him home with us and put him in the ground beside Papa in Saint Wendel. I told him so quite weepily, as if he were standing there beside me, and right away I heard my big brother answer in my head—"Stop that foolishness right now Lucy, I'm doing just fine here with Papa's people." He always was a straight talker, but I don't know that could have been true, because he only ever knew about ten words of French.

Anyhow, after so much anticipation about our trip of a lifetime, I wasn't expecting how I ended up feeling. Suffice to say it wasn't how I had imagined it. I had always thought I had some deep visceral connection to Europe. Instead, I had this strange feeling the whole time I was there, as if I was somehow fading, seeping away, leaching down into the ancient earth beneath my feet. Here at last was the old country, the motherland, the native soil of our tenderest, yet most tenacious roots. It echoed loudly within us, in our bones, in our skulls, in our soul space.

To it, I owed the fundamental principles of life according to which I had been raised, yet somehow something was missing. The echo came from too far away, a voice to hoarse to hear, too worn and frayed from shouting across too many miles. I felt it like a hard loss, both of us did, I think, although we didn't know quite how to talk about it. It was our trip of a life time, a substitute for the honeymoon we hadn't had, but it just wasn't how we had imagined it.

Perhaps Don and I had simply waited too many years to make the journey. The European way of life was very distant from what we were used to and the homeland was undeniably foreign to us. The American spirit dominated our habits, our rhythms, our thought-patterns, and outlook. The great European cities were incredibly beautiful, a beauty made more poignant by the countless scars left by World War II. The music was romantic. The food was wonderful and so strange. We ate such things I still couldn't tell you what they were, I don't even know how to pronounce half of them. But we, so ordinary and commonplace in Indiana, seemed loud and brash just by sitting down to a meal in Paris or Rome. It wasn't just our accents or our ideas—it was everything; our clothes, our table manners, our hairstyles, even our pearly white teeth made us seem like an invading alien species. Lucy and Don O'Grady, despite our French–German and Irish–Italian blood, truly came from a whole different world.

CHAPTER 17

I WROTE LONG LETTERS to Resy about everything that happened in Europe. I wanted her to hear the thoughts in my head. I'm not sure I explained it all properly. I can't imagine how it filtered through to her, looking at it from her perspective on a different hemisphere, she herself immersed in a totally alien culture. In those letters I promised her that I would visit her soon, but it turned out I never kept my promise. One thing or another, then another made it impossible. It was never the right time, something always seemed to come up. Why did I say that? It's not true, it's just what I tell myself, but today is not the day for fibbing or polite concoctions. The truth is that I hated Australia for how it seemed to enchant her, how it stole her from me. I certainly felt no great love for Mr. Coleman either. A dumb part of me even felt that if I went there then she would never have any reason to come back home, and an even dumber part probably thought it was a way to punish her for leaving us and all the pain she caused. It was my silent protest I suppose. I know now that I was a fool, that I let the worst parts of myself control me, because indulging my pain and self-pity had weakened my character. I should not have allowed that to happen. I should have overcome my pettiness. This remains my deepest regret, my greatest error.

Resy was the mother of two adorable baby boys, Mark and Mike. Though we had never seen them, or kissed them, or smelt them, or rocked them to sleep, we were still thrilled to be grandparents and always had a little album of photographs at the ready to bore our friends and neighbors with. Mark and Mike grew up to become two dashing Australian gentlemen I barely knew. In fact, I only had the privilege of meeting them in person recently. They were handsome, well-mannered, and talked with quite an accent, so I had trouble understanding them at times. I just loved to look at them though, finding hints of Resy in everything they did, even their tiniest movements or mannerisms. Had I been afraid, all this time, of seeing only Bill in them? Had such a silly thought robbed me of whole decades with those adorable boys in my life? It's a horrid idea, I admit, that I could have been so prejudiced. As it happened, they were still only children when they lost their mother, and Bill remarried and formed a new family so quickly that there was little opportunity for them to stay in touch.

Once I had gotten to know them a little better, they told me of a funny promise Resy had made them make before she died, and I suppose it was the real reason they finally made their pilgrimage to Evansville: that if I ever ended up old and alone, they would come and take me away to live with them in Australia! I could hardly contain my laughter when they told me that, it was a crazy idea of course, but it did my heart a world of good to know my sweet, sweet Resy had thought of me, even when she realized her own time was running out. In some automatic, abstract way, I loved these nice youngsters because they were my flesh and blood, though they were still strangers to me. While my love for them existed, it was superficial and untested, like the first ice on a frozen pond. We lacked those banal, intimate, direct experiences, those daily trifles that build up to something massive and solid, like my love for my children or Don.

Once they realized I wasn't going anywhere, Mark and Mike gallantly hid their relief and thought up other ways to look after me. They got me some sort of old-person alarm, with a big red button I could press to call Helen if I fell over or whatever, and they left some money to use for a nurse or any other kind of mollycoddling I might need. They were good boys, gentle-spirited like their mother, and must have made her very proud every time she looked down on them from heaven. When we said goodbye, I loved them more than I had when we'd said hello, and that was something precious to savor. They had reminded me that my heart still worked just fine. I was still able to give and receive love, even after so many losses. In their eyes and their smiles, especially Mark's, I saw my beloved Resy one last time. But hold on just a minute—did I tell you about Bernie yet? His story happened well before I met my grandsons!

Why is everything running together in my head? My little lion cub deserves more time surely? More words at least, if time is now beyond my grasp. I had plenty of time with him his first two summers, not like with Mark and Mike. Please Lord let me remember him one last time, he was so precious to me. You really must know that Bernie was absolutely adorable as a baby—he had the same unruly head of strawberry blond curls as his mother Brenda, and a generous dusting of cinnamon freckles just like his namesake Bernard. He also had Papa's sunny disposition and sensitive nature. I used to love cuddling him and telling him stories of his brave grandfather sailing the high seas and all but discovering America single-handedly. Often, when I cradled him to sleep, I would keep holding him long after he had drifted off, just breathing in his hypnotic scent. He smelt like Grandma's special Christmas cookies dipped in warm milk, and what I think was just pure, unadulterated goodness. I saw him every chance I could. Watching him grow was like looking into a fairground mirror where I could somehow catch sideways glimpses of how my own father might have been as a little boy—such is the magic of children and the powerful spells they unknowingly cast. I don't know exactly when that magic wears off, but I know it happens much too soon, leaving a permanent imprint on our hearts.

As a young man it would turn out that Bernie loved to travel, and he was the only one who tried to keep something of our European roots alive within him, as I had in my time. He studied Spanish at high school, but he also taught himself to speak French fluently and had an innate affinity for the language. At university he chose medicine, and to our immense pride became a capable and well-respected family doctor. Never losing his ready smile, he later dedicated his life to helping the poor and the sick in the Chicago suburbs, where he eventually settled after many adventures around the world. During his visits to his creaky old aunt, I would always ask him to tell me about his trips to France, about the wonders he had seen in Paris, the City of Light, those were my favorite stories. Wherever he went, he never forgot to send me a postcard. I always put them up on the refrigerator with a magnet, sometimes turning the picture side out, but more often with the writing, so I could hear his voice every time I read his usual sign-off, always in French to indulge our shared pleasure: *"Ma chére tata, je suis ton Bernard."*

When his nation called, Bernie served as a military doctor and was decorated. It was one of the moments he was proudest to share with us, saying it was an honor he accepted on behalf of our whole family, in recognition of the contribution each of us made to the man he became. However, he had his dark times, too, as even the most successful people do. He married a woman named Suzanne who sadly died in a car accident shortly afterwards, and they never had the chance to start a family. It destroyed my poor nephew; he just couldn't make sense of such a tragic loss. In desperate pain, he took to the bottle, and to pills, and for many months nothing we did or said seemed to make any difference. Luckily, a friend of his who had survived his own struggles with sobriety eventually managed to bring him out of it. Little by little he transformed his angst into positive energy that became the new driving force in his life. He found a way to go on by dedicating himself body and soul to the service of others, the only cure that could counteract his self-destructive urges. He made a conscious, determined choice to resist, to keep his head above water instead of letting himself sink, unlike his grandfather. Papa had died of a broken heart, drowning in the sorrowful loss of Jonathan, but my nephew managed to restrain his demons for many years.

While he was getting back on his feet, Bernie decided to come and live with my husband and I for a while: they were good days. My little lion cub, just like Papa, was a wonderful storyteller and we learned a lot about the many parts of the world through him. After that period, we rarely saw him, because he was always keeping busy with one project or another, unleashing all the love he would have given his beloved Suzanne onto his patients. Even if he wasn't nearby, we knew he was doing well and making us proud. We had to accept that constant action had become essential to his stability—from an addict he had become a compulsive do-gooder. Sadly, he left this world at just sixty-one, such a young age, still with a dozen projects on the go, still struggling onward. Though my years by then weighed heavily on my bones, I accompanied him on foot from the church to the cemetery. As his coffin was lowered into the ground, I again felt the pain of a child being torn from me. I was alone.

Though there were many mourners, there were no other relatives at the burial in Chicago that day. I had no one to lean on, or to comfort me if I collapsed. So instead of letting myself go, I bore the immense suffering in respectful silence, muted by death, its infinite void, by what I have always secretly called the Mystery. Once I got home, I opened my well-worn photo album and began to pull out all the special pictures, then I taped them up on my bedroom walls so I wouldn't feel so alone, not caring one bit for the paintwork. I chose to believe, of course, that my loved ones were in that other place together, watching over me— the place of the Mystery. Almost all my family, all the loved ones I had somehow outlived. I prayed for them out loud, one at a time, at the top of my voice, almost shouting, not whispering like I usually did. After a time, I received an answer in the form of a sudden feeling that came over me: everything was as it should be, as God had set out. We had reached an understanding. Bernie's death was classified as an accidental overdose, and so he was able to have a proper church funeral and burial. Those were different times, less enlightened, less forgiving. Even now I can barely admit to myself that he most likely took his own life, whether by accident or design. He was a practicing Catholic like me, so I fear for his soul and he must have too of course.

Where is he now? Was he in his right mind? What could have driven him to do something so monstrous after so many sober years? Did he really know what he was doing? Was this his first relapse or had there been others? Could he really have harmed himself, knowing how much he was still capable of doing in this world, and knowing how precious he was to me, and how bereft I would be? I had thought he trusted me, that he would come to me for comfort if he needed it. Was this just a vanity of mine? Or an excuse? I should have meddled more, paid more attention to him, demanded more attention from him. It hadn't even occurred to me that he might never have felt safe, or loved, or complete again after Suzanne or that his years in the military had scarred him far more deeply than he ever let on. Was he terrified of aging, nearing retirement and no longer having his work to keep him occupied, and thus keep his demons at bay? I had chosen to believe that old nonsense of "time heals," though I knew otherwise. I never dug far enough beneath the surface—the usual molehills of boundaries, privacy and superficiality that we make mountains of when it suits us. Could his story have ended better if I had done better as his aunt? I'll never know and that is my punishment.

These are mysteries we cannot resolve even from the afterlife; beneath the surface of every being lies a layer of emotions that no one else can comprehend. It's that very layer of stuff that makes sense of every life and every gesture. Discovering that life possesses us, (not the other way around), is a hard realization and requires true courage to grasp. Once you accept this fact, it shakes your soul to its very roots, and lays all your weaknesses bare. Was it too much for Bernie, alone in such dark water? Perhaps he couldn't bear the weight of his grieving soul any longer. Had he lost himself in the pursuit of a series of obsessions which fatally eroded his will to live? Sometimes I fear the weight could be too heavy for many of this younger generation, grown as they were on such flimsy foundations and with such shallow, stunted roots. Nowadays youngsters live in their heads, they have retreated into their minds and emotions, shrunken away from their bodies and souls. Rarely do they let their bare feet sink down into the damp raw earth or let the cold stars or the white dawn light penetrate deep into their eyes. It has become fashionable to say that judgement is a bad thing, but tell me, in a world where only thoughts and sensations and feelings are given importance, with no discernment, no judgement, no fear of being judged, no sense of being part of the greater universe: how do we navigate? We cannot choose a direction if we have been deprived of our moral compass. Only discipline and discernment can give our existence here on earth any meaningful consistency.

CHAPTER 18

I REMAIN LUCY BELMONT. No one is coming. Time is passing, or perhaps there is no more time where I am now? There's that faint whirring again, sometimes I think I can hear my heart beat, unless I'm imagining it, unless it's my alarm clock ticking. What if it turns out I'm still alive after all? I'm not sure it would make a difference any more, one way or another.

Time. First, I lost my father well before his time, then I didn't get to enjoy my own children for long, and then I barely had even a moment with my grandsons, or so it seems to me now. Was it all my fault? Did I squander my time or did I live it well? Did I try hard enough to make my life special? Did my poor dear father let go of life so soon because I simply wasn't special enough to make up for the loss of his firstborn son? These ugly thoughts come to the surface sometimes when I let my guard down and don't keep busy. Floundering about in a sea of self-pity does nobody any good, and all this time I'm floating in right now isn't helping—why am I stuck here? To torment me? Was I not enough for my own children? Is that why Resy never brought her boys to me? Is this my punishment? I must stop this wallowing right now! After all you didn't just hop on a plane those days, Australia was another planet almost. I know I wasn't perfect, I wasn't your typical mother-hen type, that's for sure, but I loved my children with all my heart.

I don't know how Greg and Resy would judge my participation in their adult lives—"telephonic" . . . "postal" perhaps? I made a mess of it, that's the truth. We did have many wonderful moments together when they were young, despite everything that came after. Our small world was a delightful place. We always took our time with things when they were little, and even before Green River Road developed, we found plenty to do. It wasn't hard to get around the center of Evansville in those days. We went about on foot or on the city trolleys, and of course parking a car wasn't a big deal like it is now. We took long, idle walks in Sunset Park, following the river path with Resy in the stroller and Greg's tiny hand in mine. I loved watching him wobbling along, stopping a million times to feed the ducks or throw rocks in the water and count the ripples. There was always something new for families and lots of moms and babies about—this was the burgeoning River City after all. I remember when the carousel came to the Mesker Park Zoo, it had sixty-eight glorious hand-carved horses and I promise you my babies rode each and every one of them at least twice. Then there were our special picnics in Garvin's Grove, special because we invited very important guests—usually Greg's stuffed monkey Bobo and whatever doll Resy's favorite was that day. Laden with blankets, treats and toys, we'd select a nice broad tree and spread out our feast in its cool shade. When we were full to the brim, we'd lie back to watch the branches swaying above us, and try to tempt the sparrows and the squirrels with our leftovers.

All three of us loved being outdoors, and that was one of our happiest places. I heard it's gotten run down over the years, but once upon a time Garvin's Park really was very special. It opened not long before Mama and I moved to Evansville, and I still remember our first visit like it was yesterday. We were still nostalgic for the farm, but we truly felt lost in nature again just as soon as we went through the gates. They'd planted a long row of giant oaks all along the west side to screen off the factory district, and there were masses of shrubs and curving wooded paths so you barely noticed the city in the background, whichever way you looked. It was a feast for the ears too! There was a pretty, tinkling fountain that the birds drank out of, and the best part was the Evansmere—a great big pond with all sorts of fish, frogs and turtles. When you closed your eyes there was a concert of birdsong, and trilling, and chirping, and croaking—it was just like being out in the countryside. There was a time when you felt looked after, living here in Evansville. They put thought, time, and consideration into planning things properly, and it made all the difference.

Naturally, we kept our big family adventures for Sundays, so that Don could come. Those were some of our best moments as parents, I think. We taught the kids to swim in the warm, buoyant water of the Fritzlar Salt Baths, and to ice skate on Sweetser Pond, near the mouth of Pigeon Creek. Back then it always seemed to freeze over just in time for the holidays. We spent a lot of time outdoors, in the woods or on the water, all year round. Did you know people used to call Evansville the barbecue capital of the USA? It seemed that way at my house, at least. Dan would light the grill in almost any weather, and the kids loved his cooking, as did our neighbors. A friend of ours used to deliver the juiciest steaks right to our door, and stay for dinner as often as not. The food back then was out of this world, let me tell you. There were all sorts of eateries in town, and many very fine places to dine, but The Honey Fluff Do-nut shop was my little Greg's Mecca, and I was quite partial to a caramel long john myself. Do they still make them? Some things never change, I still love my treats, and my fun-filled hometown, but even boring rainy evenings at home were special now I look back . . . just watching the children play jacks or pick up sticks, or make models on the coffee table as a jolly fire burned in the hearth, logs chopped in our own backyard, it was all heaven. Have I been in and out of heaven all along, without even noticing it?

When Resy and Greg were a bit older, we began taking them on day trips, whenever Don wasn't too tired or achy. Luckily, he had taught me to drive shortly after we were married, and I had my license. You'll think it odd, but most of my lady friends still didn't have much interest in driving back then. The children's absolute favorite thing was a visit to the lovely old village of New Harmony. It was a long drive but we'd pack sandwiches and root beer, and stop by the roadside for a picnic whenever we felt like it. If you ever get the chance to visit you should jump at it. The prettiest month is June, when the gorgeous Trees of the Golden Rain are in bloom. October is a real treat too, with the beech and maple and gum and hickory all aflame in the blue haze that rises from the Wabash. Remember to look up from time to time if you're walking along the trails down to the riverbank—once we saw an eagle's nest in one of the tall trees above us. It's a village of wonders that way, and somehow time loses all meaning there.

Nothing is what you'd expect to come across in Posey County, or anywhere else for that matter—from the Roofless Church, to the granary that doubled as a fortress, to the two mysterious labyrinths. It hardly seems possible to think all that was created for a single goal—the pursuit of betterment. Could such a thing happen nowadays, for all our supposed sophistication? The children loved to play in what they called the maze. Sometimes it was impossible to drag them away until the sun was low on the horizon, and we'd head home exhausted, accompanied by the blinking glow of the first fireflies. I remember one birthday Helen gave me a book all about the history of the Harmonists and their celestial pursuits—I would have been well in my sixties by then so I don't remember who the author was, but he wrote that the journey to New Harmony is measured in years as well as miles, in timelessness as well as time. Now I can say, at last, I know exactly what he meant, back then I still didn't have a clue.

As the kids became teens we stopped going so much. I guess they had a world of thrills just outside their garden gate—Green River Road's transformation from dirt road into Evansville's prime entertainment district was already well underway. They could just walk outside and find something new—record stores, burger joints, even a drive-in movie theatre. As the years passed, they saw it all arrive; soda fountains and malt shops, the first 3D films, color TV, polaroid cameras, new ways to have fun like roller-skating or discos. Their most ordinary toys would have seemed like miracles to me at their age, and I wonder what would I have thought of Resy's view-master back in Saint Wendel? What passed for fun on the farm was very different indeed—we had some games of course, like marbles, and baseball, and my brothers had a sled, but mostly we just entertained ourselves.

You might think there wasn't so much for a girl to do but I played cards with Mama and Grandma, and we did things like darning and washing and baking together. We had all kinds of tender little animals that needed care and nursing from time to time—kittens, lambs, calves, chicks, ducklings, piglets and even a foal once. There was always such a lot to be done; fetching water from the well, harvesting, milking, threshing, butchering—it went on from dawn till dusk and it changed every season. One of the best times I remember might seem like nothing to you now, but one year there was a bumper crop of melons, they were huge and sweet, and suddenly the whole village was harvesting them all together. We ate melons for weeks on end, and none of us minded one bit! I really don't remember having any toys except a little ragdoll, Dot. Grandma Gretel made her specially for me; she had braids and wore a smock just like mine, and mostly lived contentedly, in my apron pocket. I don't remember ever wanting another toy, or being bored, or even hearing that word used much, usually we were all worn out by evening and fell asleep as soon as our heads hit the pillow.

Things change of course, but other things stay the same. Like Papa and Johnny, Greg was still a very young man when he struck out in the world, leaving our little haven on the now chaotic Green River Road behind him. Before long, we were only vaguely acquainted with the details of his everyday life, his work, and relationships. When we spoke on the phone I didn't know where to imagine him, couldn't picture what chair he was sitting in or what shirt he was wearing. I lacked details, knowledge, trivia, minutiae—time in other words, time together. I didn't even understand why he didn't want to settle down and raise a family. When I asked about it, he would say that his career was too demanding and that he was always on the road, that it wouldn't be right to have children just to leave them without a father. He had made the choice to dedicate his life to his artistic vocation and that made him grow into a coherent, responsible young man.

It did eventually dawn on me that he might be a homosexual, but just thinking about the word embarrassed me, and there was no way I could have brought myself to say it out loud to my own child. Aside from my embarrassment there was still the legal aspect to consider, and his reputation at work, and I don't know if he could have continued attending church. Who could I have asked such questions to back then? It was overwhelming to think about the repercussions, even if I had by some miracle found the words to broach the subject. Then again, Greg was often surrounded by women and had plenty of friends, so I managed to convince myself that he was still sowing his wild oats, or that he simply hadn't met "the one" yet. Did I make enough of the time I had with Greg? At least I managed to imbue him with my wanderlust and eagerness to explore, we had that passion to share. My eyes looked through his every visit he made to far-off places all around the globe with his music.

As he matured artistically, Greg began to record more and more classical works, and I loved all that. I used to listen to his Mozart sonatas every evening, playing them loud on the living room stereo, as I sat alone in the kitchen after clearing up. That way it was easier to pretend my son was actually still home with us, seated at his piano in the other room. A way to claw back some time with him. Don used to say this little ritual of mine was just sentimental nonsense, but he would always stay tucked away in his armchair facing the hearth while the Greg's music was playing, so I wouldn't see his eyes misting up.

CHAPTER 19

As PARENTS WE WERE closer to Resy than to Greg. Is it wrong to say it if it's the truth? Is it something that happens with boys, that you have less fear when they go out into the world? Or was it because of the unspoken secret between us? It doesn't mean we loved her more, perhaps we simply couldn't ever have imagined that our lives could go on without her. When she left for Australia, she was still just a child in our eyes, not remotely conscious that she had robbed us of the future we had envisioned for our family; watching her become a woman, helping her raise our grandchildren, decades and decades growing older and wiser, creakier and crankier together, our bond only getting stronger every year. It was not to be. We had taken so much for granted; and it had been a terrible miscalculation.

Somehow, we cobbled together a makeshift relationship with our grandsons through photographs, letters, and occasional crackly phone calls. Resy and I wrote, and I always kept her up to date on all the happenings and gossip around Evansville, trying to tempt her back by stoking her homesickness. I wrote every tiny detail about our family and all my plans, and hopes. I wanted her to be proud of how we were managing without her, how her father had managed to transform his disability into motivation, and was getting fitter and stronger than ever. In return, she wrote about the infinite landscapes of Australia, and the endless whirlwind of novelties her new home offered; words, foods, shoes, animals, bugs—everything was different there. By and by, her descriptions became almost mystical; it seemed the place had something that drew her in, something she felt in her soul. I thought I was losing even more of her, that her fondness for her native land was fading. I couldn't have guessed the real reason for her new-found spirituality.

She understood all about time, better than any of us. Whenever I get low, thinking about how my *too* long life meant I outlived my own beloved children, I think of what Resy faced so bravely, and it snaps me right out of it. She never told me about the horrible illness that had gripped her when she was still so young. I never suspected anything. She must have known long before she died that she was destined to leave her two boys still just defenseless children. She did her best to prepare them, even left them letters and birthday cards that she entrusted to her husband so that they would never feel like she was gone altogether. I understand now that she was attempting to imprint some trace of herself on the future. Most often though, when I think of her, I find myself being sucked back many decades into the past. Suddenly, I have my beautiful new baby girl again, I can smell her, I can feel her in my arms. Her wispy, hazelnut hair is sticking out like a cloud around her head—her halo I used to say jokingly. My angel. Her life was the blink of an eye, and yet her death is an eternity that still lives inside me.

Some things I did read between the lines of her letters—that her marriage was not always a happy one, for example, but they were different times, and I didn't want to pry. Bill had a successful career as a manager for a major multinational and was often away on business, while she stayed home raising her boys, as was expected. Maybe that's how they grew apart. Is that why she never insisted I came for a visit? Was she afraid I would judge or meddle in their relationship? Or did she just want me to be proud like always, and spare me any worry—after all, what could I really have done being so far away? I wish I had been there for my grandchildren. The boys were Resy's pride and joy. Mark loved to sail and even won some junior races. We put a big, framed photograph of one of his wins right in the hallway of our home, so it was the first thing we saw when we opened the front door. Don would always point it out to every new visitor, he loved boasting of his talented grandson. It was our way of fooling ourselves that we knew that beaming boy we had never actually met in person.

At times I like to rake myself over the coals, wondering how I could have been a better mother, wondering how things might have been different. I won't do it again now, let's just say I think the best thing I did was to imbue my children with our family values, which were always our touchstones, our pillars of strength. That was how I equipped them for the paths they later chose to travel. I don't think I did wrong, yet sometimes it felt like I was being punished. I never could have imagined what evil would befall me, that I would outlive them, that both my babies would die before me, and without me. I was not there for them even in death, and right to the end they both kept secrets from me. When, after years of foolery, my weasel of a son-in-law finally revealed to me that Resy was in fact at death's door, Don was confined to a hospital bed and nearing his own end. I had to choose who to be with. Why such a cruel fate?

A very sad November day I journeyed in my mind to rejoin my daughter at long last. I walked with her beside her coffin, lay alongside her in the grave and I left this world for a period. Meanwhile my body sat inert beside my husband's bed, leaking tears, unnoticed, her sodden photograph clutched in my numb fist. Time did not pass, time did not heal. "Out of sight, out of mind"—sometimes what we think is a proverb is really just a sick joke. "Out of sight, our heart devours itself" they should say. I last held Resy in my arms when she was still young and beautiful and ready to depart on her big adventure. It was her first time taking an airplane, and it was something unimaginably rare and glamourous back then—the tickets were a wedding gift from her posh new in-laws, of course. She looked every inch the blushing bride, her hair rolled up, her lips reddened, and she was wearing her best outfit, naturally, her lilac-colored honeymoon suit. I tried to fix that image in my mind, our last moment together: a lovely, smiling girl, so pretty I could barely believe she was mine.

Why hadn't she told me? That question has been my constant torment ever since. Her death was such a devastating blow that when I resurfaced from my grieving, I had aged many years in a just a few weeks. I was frail now, vulnerable. I was still alive, though, and finally resigned to accept my fate or perhaps my punishment. I went on because life is a gift we cannot return, and consciousness in physical form cannot exist without suffering. We are here to learn how not to close our eyes to suffering, but instead to live every experience that comes, until our last breath. This was my life, the time I had been allotted, the length of thread that was measured out and cut for me. Its length was not for me to know. For better or for worse, and I was still learning the lesson of how to transform suffering into a deeper way of existing, a new awareness.

Helen was always by my side, trying to patch up my wounds, keep my heart beating, but nothing can dull the indescribable pain of losing one's own child. My father had known this, and now I knew it too. There are varying degrees of loss, each requiring different skills to survive, but the loss of my daughter . . . that was an abomination to me. It started a voiceless screaming inside my head, and for a long time I contemplated my own death, even yearning for it. Nevertheless, year after year, on I went. I continued to age, seeing friends, relatives, even some of my old students go to their reward in heaven while I was left behind. I survived, a somewhat decrepit but substantially healthy witness to the empty spaces their departures created. Should I have drowned in grief? My faith alone kept me afloat, made me certain I would see them all again.

Months, weeks, days, hours, minutes, seconds seemed to drag monotonously, yet the outside world was changing, getting harsher all the while, just as the swinging sixties had dwindled into the soulless seventies. It got so I couldn't even bear to watch the evening news, more often than not. Those were hard times for many, marked by different kinds of pain: it seemed like wave after wave of drugs and violence were sweeping across America, the hippy movement blundered along in its own confused way, and a generation of young men were obliterated by Vietnam. Why did every generation have to pay its blood tribute to these senseless, abstract, foreign wars? Time took almost everyone from me, eventually even Bernie, though he left the military intact. I'll never forget the last hug I gave my nephew; he should have lived so much longer. Relentlessly, my life continued on, after every loss, every dark winter, and just as inevitably each spring my garden blossomed anew, full of the sap-green scent of fresh promise.

Despite all the grief and misfortune around me, it seemed that I, Lucy Belmont, was destined to grow stronger, more robust in spirit, as month after month went by. To my surprise, I managed to stay relatively positive, find some moments of serenity, and gradually accept that I was returning to life. One day Helen brought me a visitor who was my grandniece. Just think, I had a grandniece I didn't even remember I had.

Tell no one, I beg you, they'll think I'm cuckoo, but the truth is I haven't been able to keep my extended family straight in my head for about two decades now. Turned out I hadn't seen this one since she was a toddler. Eddie's son Robert had had two children, and here was the girl, all grown up. Where does the time go? Her name was Barbara, and she was a pretty one, alright.

Sadly, Helen told me, she had turned rebellious and fallen in with the wrong crowd while she was away at college. As they often do, things went from bad to worse: she had got caught up with drugs, and then found herself with child. Her poor father was scandalized and had disowned her after a huge hullabaloo, so now she had taken refuge with her Aunt Helen, hoping she would help her pay for an abortion. Her wise auntie, though, was determined to sort out the mess her own way. I found myself witnessing the drama of Barbara's generation unfolding right in my living room. What could I do? I told my grandniece the story of her great-grandparents, wanting her to feel she, too, had the strength of our proud ancestors who had been so forthright, devout, and generous despite their many hardships. Barbara seemed all mixed up at first, but as we spoke, I realized that her temporary confusion masked a real aspiration: she had a dream, she wanted to make something of herself.

What she utterly lacked, however, was encouragement and direction. This lack had dug a deep, dark well of uncertainty within her, and now it was brimming with self-doubt, distorting how she saw herself. We talked about love—how can you love, and at the same time plan to take a life? I couldn't find the right words to tell her what I was feeling, so instead I gave her a present; the wooden nest that her grandfather Edward had carved many, many years earlier. She was moved, her eyes shone as she sat holding it in her lap, perhaps it communicated with her better than I could myself. In the end, she decided to keep her baby, and called him David. She and her son lived with Helen for a couple of years, before she met and married Gary. Eddie had put five little birds in his nest, and it was a good omen; Barbara became the loving mother of five splendid children. She and Gary moved to Arkansas and we eventually lost touch, but I know she patched up her relationship with her father, and I believe he went to live with her when he was getting on in years.

Barbara's story had a happy ending. I wish they all did. To me, it represents a concrete example of a time good intentions led to good outcomes—perhaps it helps me keep up my belief in divine providence. Our destinies can be grand and generous if we can just keep our divine spark alive. Things can work out for the best and it's not always all doom and gloom like what I read in the newspapers. For example, even though I consider myself a Democrat, I could never accept the idea of unlimited access to abortion. Although it took me decades, I did manage to stretch my mind around divorce, intended perhaps as a consequence of a chain of mishaps and the loss of the fundamental value of patience in society today, but the act of aborting a baby is a bridge too far for me.

We don't own life. We are not the masters of it: life itself is our master. When the precautions our intelligence provides us with aren't enough, when an accident or something unintended happens, this is a sign that the mystery of life is sending us, this mystery always has meaning and reason, even if it takes time to reveal itself, even generations of time. Our true nature is to cherish life whatever its origin, not destroy it. Sadly, I am dying at the very end of the twentieth century, while the world is still weighed downed by a force of ego that goes against our natural instinct for love, and many good precepts have been intentionally destroyed or derided. I know you'll think I judge, but if I can't tell the truth now, in my last moments, when will I? How would I value my life if I had lived it without conscience, without ethics, and without discernment, without sacrifice, especially during the hardest times?

Helen and I often talked about the worrying traits we saw emerging in society. Even from my sheltered standpoint, I noticed that much of the younger generation hadn't evolved culturally, instead they had become unshakably passive; herds of vague, meandering creatures only able to obey, to follow the piper's tune mindlessly, never knowing the satisfaction of taking responsibility for their actions or having an initiative of their own. What had dimmed their spark? There was no light in their eyes and I, though much older, felt a million times more vital and lively by comparison. They were the real old folks. Admittedly, I was not out and about as much in my final few years, but what I saw happening around me was a cause for concern. I questioned Helen about what she thought of the older generations too, and she reluctantly confessed that when she observed them in town or at the mall, she often felt the urge to turn away: she saw elderly people wandering about aimlessly, or sitting and just staring at nothing, stiff, withered and impoverished by their lack of personal judgement.

What do I mean by that? Well, what would have become of me if I had let myself go like that at sixty-five or seventy or eighty? I might have wasted decades of existence to come, simply by giving up too early. I could easily have decided, at seventy let's say, to stop making an effort—and then sat around atrophying for the next twenty-seven years! What if I had refused to stay mentally and physically active and ceased to be of service in this world? I would have been an unbearable burden on Helen. Life must be chosen deliberately, and lived tenaciously every single day. Every morning we actually succeed in waking up and getting out of bed should be celebrated—it is a prize, a trophy, a reward. It is another chance to exist, to fulfill our purpose, to honor ourselves or our families, to feel joy or curiosity or gratitude, and most importantly to merit another awakening tomorrow. I'm disappointed to see that so many older people seem to have lost the verve of their hardy forebearers, who were still working the land, chopping wood, riding mules and washing in the river at a ripe old age.

Nowadays instead, every miniscule opportunity for exertion of any kind is avoided, and many individuals, decades younger than I am, barely even make the effort to feed or dress themselves properly anymore—leisure suits and TV dinners have siphoned off their life force, and consequently even gentle gardening or household chores are considered too much. Spoon-fed and babied, their minds also regress, often irretrievably. The youngsters are no better off, though I tend to make more excuses for them. The cold reality was already glaringly evident quite a few years ago, when Helen took me on our last Christmas shopping trip. I saw how they dragged themselves around the mall sluggishly, like bees drowning in honey; heads limp, mouths slack and expressionless. They wore bizarre and uncomfortable looking outfits and had rings and things hanging off their faces—futile, savage ornaments. Then, of course, there were the obese on their scooters, who had transformed their anger into mass so that almost any independent movement was impeded. Dear Father in heaven help us.

The rest of the crowd slipped by me fast, like minnows, never looking around them, no time to spare I suppose. When did this become acceptable? When did people stop noticing each other, stop talking, stop connecting? Are they so afraid of being accused of something that they've forgotten what basic standards of behavior are? That's tyranny. A tyranny of the banal and the soulless. Lately, our society has been manifesting signs of grave imbalance that must be addressed if it is to have any chance at a decent future. This lop-sided forward hobble is not progress, it is merely day-to-day survival. Someone must do something right now to restore our equilibrium, before the old ways are forgotten all together. Someone must find the trail of crumbs, lead us back out of the woods before the last light fades, but who will do this?

What began this downward spiral I'm not sure, but it strikes me now that many people have been undone by an excess of convenience and leisure. While removing the effort from daily existence, all the pleasure and satisfaction seems to have been drained away with it. These were the everyday achievements of making one's own bed or tying one's own shoelaces that were the first building blocks of every child's most basic self-esteem, the low-hanging fruit, the small wins that built to greater daring and greater confidence in life. Nowadays, unearthly virtual pursuits have created a jaded, disjointed society of enervated, anesthetized, and often timid or timorous beings. The value of work has been eroded and replaced with abstract simulations like hobbies. Oh yes, our pleasant hobbies seem to make life more fun, but what are they distracting us from, who are they really serving? Was there ever a worse word invented than "pastime"?

Why should I wish to merely pass my time, dribble it away uselessly, rather than take advantage of it and make it serve my highest goals? Is time not the most precious, most finite gift that the universe presents to each of us? A day has twenty-four hours for all of us, in equal and exact measure. Excessive time-wasting with hobbies subtracts energy from real, concrete work, making the worker mediocre, depriving them of the opportunity of developing ambition or pride. Moreover, since a hobby rarely produces an economic benefit, it rarely acts as a stimulus for growth. Instead, the hobbyist settles for familiar appreciation and gradually loses interest. Hobbies are sedatives for the soul, they shush the voice of our true desires and aspirations, snuff out our will to progress, and "protect" us from the natural urge to dig deep and find the courage to live up to our full potential, so we never have to measure ourselves out in the real world. Beware of pastimes, even reading.

CHAPTER 20

My name is Lucy Belmont, I'm ninety-seven years old and I lived in the house on the corner of Green River Road and Morgan Avenue for the best part of a century. I've been dead for three days but nobody's noticed yet.

My whole life I believed in miracles and now I'm genuinely hoping for one, because I don't understand what's happening to me. I've been talking about myself, or to myself, for a long time. It's quieter now, but I still hear the gentle whirring. There's a wondrous tranquility here; I feel no pain at all now, just calm. I wish my children were here with me. I'd like to lie down with them in the shady grass and watch the trees swaying their branches above us, like we used to when they were very little. I want to hear the leaves whispering and make believe that they're telling me their secrets. I used to make up fairytales for my babies from those secret words. Whisper, murmur, rustle, susurrate, dappled, adumbral, umbrageous—are those real words or just odd sounds that I'm inventing? I like the sound of some words so much better than others, autumn sounds better than fall, no one sounds better than none. But I'm tired of words now, tired of being indoors, I long to feel the soft river breeze on my body, I miss the very air I used to breathe in Evansville in my youth. I miss the cool, dry gusts that swept down from the north and the warm wet summer wind that drifted up from the south. Days upon days have passed me by, big things happening out there, changes, joys, hurts, but now that I think back on it, what really gave a meaning to my life was my inner world.

In a funny way it seems to me now like a kind of immortality, I still hear the same voice in my head that I heard a decade ago, or five decades ago, or even nine. This inner voice hasn't aged, it was my gift, given to me by God and the universe, and I cultivated it instinctively, following the guidance of my heart and my spirit. This went on every day of my life, right now too, it continues unchanged, only ever heard by me, whether I'm alive or dead . . . perhaps it even existed before I was born. My inner voice excelled in art of transforming every experience into an emotion, thus I was able to understand it and even learn from it wherever possible. Life flows through us like an underground river, whispering, daring us to uncover its hidden intent, to wonder at its depths, to savor it. I have travelled very far within myself. I have been an ancient witness to the life of my dearest Evansville. I have seen this gracious town evolve, seen all sorts of whatnot spring up—golf courses, malls, countless stores selling ever finer, ever crazier things; lately they even opened a casino where over a thousand people work, and so both prosperity and vice have come back to the center. The good and the bad inextricably bound, riches with poverty, sickness with health, like a marriage, like everything, like always. I once had more friends around my age, but I lost track of them over the years, they grew silent or were shut away.

But I'm rambling again, what is this heaviness I feel, this sadness? It's a memory, a time I don't want to return to with you, but I must. Eventually the dreadful day came when Don was taken from me. I should have been expecting it, the doctors had prepared us for the worst, but I guess I just thought it wouldn't happen so fast. It didn't seem fair to me—we should have had no worries at all at our age, after a lifetime of hard work, saving and planning. I had imagined us living out a fantasy in our golden years—reunited with the kids and grandkids, lounging on a beach in Florida or learning golf. We had sold the gas station and a good part of the land alongside our house so, with our nest egg plumped up, we could have afforded to spoil ourselves and live abundantly to a ripe old age. For this loss I was at least present, and I knew what was happening. Most importantly, we had time to say our goodbyes properly, this was a great mercy.

He was suffering, and in and out of consciousness, but when he was lucid he said some beautiful things to me. In those final days he praised me for having kept it together all these years, for having kept my dignity and refinement, for having been a faithful wife. He thanked me for all sorts of things I'd completely forgotten, even for our arguments, for not taking any nonsense, for helping him keep a level head after the amputation. Above all, he said, he was grateful to me for putting up with him, for ignoring his weaknesses, and for having stuck with him even during his worst times. He said he was sorry for so many things, but I wasn't sorry at all anymore; I was grateful for each of those hard times because they had forged us, tempered us, and made us stronger. Every trial we overcame was just another proof of our enduring love. I could barely speak without sobbing, the lump in my throat was too strong, but I think he could read it in my eyes. As broken as I was after Resy, and silently drowning in a tumult of emotions, our bond was still solid, in spite of everything.

I told him I could see his spirit clearly, as clearly as the very first day we met, and that I loved him, and that we would always be together in our hearts. He was dearer to me than ever in those final days, though in ways I was unable to express. I wanted to thank him for the wonderful life he had provided for me, for the gift of our children, for his electrifying smile, for making my heart beat, for helping me grow into womanhood, for everything we had been through together. I was grateful even for that crazy obsession with speed that had almost destroyed him, because it had led to our first meeting. Most of all I wanted him to know that he had made me feel truly alive and truly blessed. But we didn't need words to communicate in the end, touch was enough. Our eyes and hearts were enough. We had done all we could, lived all there was for us to live, and walked the path we made together, a middle way, where our principles and values intersected. Now his time had come, and I had to go on alone. I stayed by him all night, praying. When the morning light came, he was gone. Contrary to what I had feared, I didn't panic, instead I was almost numb. All I felt were unexpected sparks of crystalline calm that kept pulsing through me for hours. I knew with absolute certainty that his soul would stay with me forever, and in the long years that followed that never changed. I could always feel his presence and talk to him any time I wanted, just as if he were right there beside me.

After the funeral, Helen spent a lot of time with me. In the evenings I would take her arm and she would lead me out into the garden to walk around the magic circle of irises. Whenever I saw the sheer perfection of those flowers, I felt reinvigorated, both in body and in spirit. I used to cut some and put them in a tall vase on the kitchen table. The sight of that beauty that lasted only a single day gave me a sense of lightness that did my heart good; it reminded me that everything passes quickly. I resolved not to let myself get into a slump. Although I was home alone most of the time, I was very particular about order and cleanliness. I made myself do plenty of little domestic tasks to stay busy and not sink into gloom. I told myself we would be reunited soon. I didn't know back then that I still had so many years of life ahead of me, so it turned out this habit of staying active really served me well. Until my ninety-first year I kept limber and did my gardening daily, though after that I left it to my housekeeper Mary, at her insistence. I still kept doing some household chores religiously—that was my exercise. Sure, I was old and achy, but I was still able to keep my home and my person neat and tidy, and I was always alert to my surroundings. These little things made all the difference.

My days were quiet then, in my final years I mean, but Mary was often about for company. I used to ask her, I'm sure quite repeatedly, if she knew any other Evansville folks my age, or thereabouts. Lucky for me she did, and she told me the stories of several locals who had breathed just as much world as I had; it surprised and reassured me to hear about them. One fine June day she even brought me a live one—an ancient fellow that I eventually recognized as Jacob, a boy who had been my neighbor and playmate in Saint Wendel. I hadn't seen or heard of him in at least fifty years. It turned out he had never moved away from the village where we were born, that he had always been there "rooted like one of the decrepit old oaks in the woods where we used to play," he joked. He had married Irene, a girl a few years younger than me, and had become the proud father of three strapping sons. Sadly, his firstborn had died in the war in Indochina, a place Jacob knew nothing of, except the name. His other two boys worked in aviation in Kansas City, so he and Irene had ended up home alone, but they never gave up farming their little corner of heaven. They had been living off their land, just as they always had, when she got sick from cancer a few years back.

He was a widower now. Recently he had been obliged to sell off most of his lot to pay the last of her medical bills. He told me a funny anecdote. One day he was sitting out on his porch, minding his own business, when his neighbor's grandson leaned over the fence and asked him if he was interested in selling his house; up he got out of his chair, shaking his walking stick, and shouted across: "Would you ask a turtle to sell his shell?" We cracked up laughing at that story, and for a moment we were just kids again, and his eyes sparkled like a child's. We talked lots more after that, about our childhood, about growing up, about how the world was turning out. When it was time for him to go, moved by so much nostalgia and so many happy memories, Jacob confessed that he had had a secret crush on me when we were youngsters. "I was in love with you for years and years, but by the time I worked up the courage to tell you, you had already chosen Don" he said. That was the last time a gentleman paid me a compliment—I'd quite forgotten what a thrill it could be!

CHAPTER 21

By THE TIME I was in my nineties the world was nearing the millennium, and Green River Road was considered Evansville's top entertainment district. My home seemed ever more isolated; a leafy islet caught in a time warp. Anachronistic. A relic from bygone days. One morning, a vivacious young man turned up on my doorstep, asking if I'd like to sell up and move to the nice new apartment complex on the banks of the Ohio River, offering nothing less fanciful than "assisted living for my silver years." I gave him my most cordial smile and uttered Jacob's laconic phrase before politely slamming my front door in his face. Why should I have wanted to move anywhere else? I still had enough money for all my necessities—my home help, health insurance, two taxi rides a month to the cemetery, and even two visits a month to my beauty parlor to take care of my hairdo and the fuzz on my chin that I was a bit ashamed of. Every single morning, I forced myself to get up at a decent hour and do my ablutions; I combed my hair, put in my tortoiseshell combs, and even added a touch of lipstick and some pink blush if I was feeling down.

Fortunately, I have always been the picture of health: leaving aside some problems with my womb after my pregnancies and a touch of arthritis, my body has always been a very strong and dependable companion. Health was one of those things Don and I didn't see eye to eye on; I was almost never sick while he had so many aches and pains after the amputation. Before his accident, my husband was lively, agile, and strong, his physique was his pride and joy. Accepting his new condition when he lost his leg was virtually impossible for him. It was no good reminding him that he was lucky to be alive, not to have been incinerated in that terrible crash, he just couldn't see it that way. My positive vision offended him, so he argued or he clammed up and refused to talk about it. I was suffering, too, because I couldn't communicate with my husband, and I had to be very understanding with him and swallow my own frustration. I shared in his pain and his anger about what had happened, but I was not willing to accept that he saw himself as cursed or worthless now. Instead, after the accident, I felt a greater nearness to him as a wife, and felt I now understood the meaning of the vows I had made before God much more fully, to stay married in the good times and the bad, in sickness and in health, and that made me stay strong and determined.

During his slow rehabilitation, I would go to the hospital every day to bring Don my usual dose of sweetness and light, comfort and joy, but more often than not he pushed me away. He thought I was only so chirpy because I really didn't understand his suffering deep down, since I myself had never been seriously ill. He was wrong though, I too have my dark thoughts, I just don't allow myself the luxury of dwelling on them too long. What were my dark thoughts then? More than once I asked myself: if this accident had happened to me, would Don have left me? I don't know the answer, it depends on too many factors, there was no point tormenting myself. I also wondered if Don's attitude was prevalently a male thing. From one of the nurses, I heard the story of Josephine, a gorgeous Evansville girl who had just recently finished school and gotten engaged to a brilliant lawyer. Shortly before the big day, Josephine was diagnosed with breast cancer and she called off the wedding. Absolutely nothing, not even the love and understanding of her fiancé, could change her mind: she could not accept herself physically after the mastectomy, nor could she allow him to accept her now that she judged herself as damaged goods. Did she carry her desperation to her last breath, leaving behind just anguish and suffering for her loved ones?

How strange human behavior can be; how fragile, irrational and unpredictable we are. It's like our gears are always getting stuck. Why are we so finnicky? Deep down the truth is known to all of us, every time you face a problem you have two choices: either you delude yourself or you face it head on. Acceptance, honesty, staying in balance—it is never easy, it must be cultivated daily, as it builds up slowly like a protective callous. The rituals that I used to divide up my day were designed to help me maintain my equilibrium. Even in my final years I made sure to be clever and deliberate about dosing the rhythms of my spirit and my body; in return for good behavior, I gave myself little rewards to motivate myself without going overboard—snippets of time allocated to watching television for example, or time with my radio, or walking in the garden. Getting outdoors every single day, whatever the weather, was essential and non-negotiable, even when I didn't have pets to get me moving.

My garden was my lifeline. I loved to follow the magic circle of irises around the old oak and potter about, just breathing in time and the seasons, letting their rhythms soak into me and strengthen me, like animals do naturally. I would notice all the things that changed from month to month, recurring little treasures; new buds, nests, curly baby leaves, insects, husks, skins, secrets and surprises. I recognized the birds in my garden, and they recognized me too. Red-crested cardinals, fluffy blue jays, doves, finches, sparrows, larks, a lone downy woodpecker, sometimes hungry little hawks—Evansville has so many birds, and I studied them all. In the summertime I would even spot the odd robin, yellow warbler, or best of all a tiny ruby-throated hummingbird. Hummingbirds bring good luck, or so it's said in these parts, and Padre Peter told me there is even a passage in the Bible about how they drink nectar, and it's a teaching about *finding strength in times of sorrow.* Isn't that the secret of life all summed up in six words? They used to teach those kinds of phrases in school once. I never would have imagined something so useful could just stop. What will happen to my birds and my garden now—will Helen keep them safe? Nowadays, I suppose most people couldn't tell a Carolina wren from a chickadee. It's such a shame, they have so much wisdom to share.

That reminds me of Grandpa Josef's tales of the far-off Alps, where birds were both a clock and a calendar, as well as a source of sustenance. Blackbirds, he said, were always the first to know when Spring was coming; their beaks would turn bright yellow, and they would sing out melodious mating calls sometimes as early as February if the weather was especially fine. When he was a young man hunting in the mountains, it would be the caws of certain crows that would tell him he was approaching a high altitude, as those particular birdcalls are only heard at four or even five thousand feet above sea level. I asked Grandpa what they sounded like—a heaven song was what he called it, because he only heard it when he was above the clouds. That was his paradise, the race track was Don's, my garden was mine. Sometimes I tried to whistle along with the songs my birds sang, but they didn't seem to appreciate it—only my old friend Mister ever took any notice. Nevertheless, there was an unspoken bond between my ever-wilder garden and I, and it only strengthened as the years passed: that was my own abundant corner of tall trees and lush greenery, hemmed in by the constant flow of traffic.

It had become an oasis for many furtive creatures, my most precious companions in my increasing solitude. We had all been left behind by the world beyond, and now I think perhaps we were the better for it. There is nothing more joyous and beautiful to see, in springtime, than the ritual dances of birds as they seek a mate and build the intricate, wondrous nests from which one day their offspring will make their first tremulous flight. When I wasn't pottering or gardening, I used to like sitting out on the porch. I was often alone, but I did have some four-legged company—did I forget to tell you that? I had a cat first and then a dog. Chou Chou the cat was a birthday gift from Helen. I'm not sure how she came up with that odd idea, but he turned out to be quite a clean and pleasant housemate, and was a calming presence in my life, if not overly affectionate. Having grown up on a farm I was quite unsentimental about pets, and it had never really occurred to me that I might enjoy having one. Chou Chou was a handsome and stately marmalade creature that I ruthlessly overfed in order to discourage any interest he might have had in my birds. He had an uneventful life, which terminated unexpectedly under a car, much to my dismay. I have to admit, had he not been so fat, he would probably have been able to avoid the accident—I hope he and Helen were able to forgive me.

My dog Mister was a whole different story. He showed up one day out of the blue, not long before Don finally went to his reward. He looked something like a Labrador, though he was certainly a mix of several breeds. We took a shine to each other instantly and spent twelve blissful years as close companions. We had a lot in common; I would potter in the garden and he would shadow me patiently. He was a curious and constant observer of the other inhabitants of my little jungle, but never harmed any living critter. He loved being petted and I loved petting him—sometimes I would hold one of his big soft furry paws in my hand, and he would gaze at me with his dark, liquid eyes and bat his long black lashes like he wanted to tell me something. He melted my heart, my Mister. You know, those eyes reminded me a lot of Don's! Now I heartily regret that I never let him into the house, not even the kitchen. I was very houseproud and I wasn't quite so nimble anymore, so I was afraid I wouldn't be able to manage cleaning up after him. Plus I was always a bit fussy about smells, and with the traffic, airing the house wasn't easy. What a dumb dodo I was to indulge such silly inclinations. Anyhow, I made him a nice warm bed on the porch as a compromise, and he was a forgiving soul, so our bond was strong despite my error.

Mister could read my mind, and my heart, and he always knew if I was anxious or under the weather. One morning, when he didn't see me coming down the stairs at the usual time, he barked and howled so loud and so long that I forced myself out of bed to see what was wrong, though I was feeling quite unwell. That was the day he saved my life, and to my mind he deserved a medal. It turned out that I'd left a gas ring on when I'd warmed up some milk the night before. Afterward, Helen had the whole house fitted with all sorts of safety gadgets and alarms and things, but I felt safe and sound as long as Mister was with me. That said, it was a wake-up call that made me realize even my time would come, sooner or later. Then came the awful day Mister disappeared, just the same way he had materialized years before, leaving a cavern of emptiness behind him. I was so distraught without his company, I vowed never to keep another pet. My heart couldn't take it, and I was getting too old.

CHAPTER 22

I WAS BORN AND remain Lucy Belmont. Is it possible to make sense of things, at last? To know why things turned out the way they did and be at peace with it all?

I wish I could tell you more about all the people who were dearest to me, I've left so much out. I guess Helen stands for all of them in a way; she somehow sums up all the nice things they did for me. She was so wise, and never stopped studying new and fascinating subjects; psychology, anthropology, religion, philosophy, the arts, culture and history of our beautiful home state. I couldn't even guess how many correspondence courses she took with USI, and she was able to handle just about anything life sent her way as a result. She was the perfect niece; she never forgot a birthday or an anniversary. Every chance she got she would stop by and say hello. She never left me. Helen was a great gift, or perhaps a reward—there, you see, that's how wonderful a person she is; she made me feel like I must have done something good to deserve her in my life. I knew this day would come eventually, so I left a letter for her in a drawer where I know she'll find it, to thank her from the bottom of my heart.

I put aside a few things for her, but not too much to overwhelm her with clutter, I hope. They are happy memories mostly, things we shared, yellowed pictures, worthless knick-knacks, aged handmade bits and bobs—but more alluring to me than a pirate's hoard. I've given her the house, of course, and what remains of the land—a couple of acres

now tragically overgrown. To my nephews in Australia, I've left nothing, because I think it would just be a nuisance to them. Now I'm not sure I did right. I don't think my few dollars or my trinkets would mean much to them, but I don't want to offend either. Anyway I trust Helen to take care of that. She knows what these surviving symbols of my time on earth signify, she will separate the totems and treasures from the trifles and find homes for what should be preserved. She helped me care for all my weird and wonderful belongings for half a lifetime at least. Notions I called them, like the things they used to sell in Kessler's Emporium.

Helen was my rock, not just my niece or my "almost daughter." I entrust to her all the sweetest juice of my late fruits, to do with as she will. My spiritual life and revelations, all my diaries, my most rebellious thoughts, my secrets, my weaknesses, my notions, my nonsense and my dreams. When I was young, I sometimes dreamt of escaping, of running away, so I wouldn't have to face my daily grind of housework, school, children, the pungent stench of petrol, Don's moods; it was my pilgrim spirit emerging from time to time. I also had a lot of repressed creativity, and I will have to admit this before God when I am judged: I squandered, even rejected that gift of his to me. Now I regret that I never searched within myself for the courage to use it. I never dared to develop it, transform it, and share it with others. I didn't cultivate my voice like my friend Amy Cox did, I didn't write books or paint or draw. Now all my reflections, my hard-won wisdom, my growth, my progress . . . all die with me. All that's left are my diaries, and I only wrote those at Helen's prompting. I'll take most of my secrets to my grave, sealed with me in my tomb like Pharoah's wives. Helen knows who the people are in all the faded pictures. It was she who wrote the names on the backs of all those photographs, laying out a sort of human patchwork quilt on the living room rug one afternoon. She will take good care of Greg's records.

Thinking of my Greg, I know I haven't said enough about him, the son who slipped through my fingers. Greg passed away from a sudden heart attack in Chicago. Only fifty-five years old, he just disappeared from my life, like the notes of a song escaping from a wireless. I got a call, out of the blue, saying that he had been carted off to the emergency room. He had never been sick, not a day in his life! While Helen and I were making our mad run to the airport, a vicious snowstorm hit Indiana and all flights were cancelled, so for a second time, I wept for a child of mine over a photograph. I listened obsessively to his music all through the night, looking for comfort that could not be found. There was no acceptance this time. Poor Greg, it seemed so unreal, I couldn't process it. Who held his hand, who closed his eyes when his soul went to God? The next day we were able to fly again, but by then I was too weak and sick to travel. I was in my eighties and the shock and the pain had been too much for me, I felt as if I had been emptied out and filled with lead overnight. I remained bedridden for several weeks, almost unable to function. Helen went to him, saw to the funeral and took care of the paperwork for his estate. She brought me back a handful of personal items and slowly helped me understand what was happening. I knew that Greg lived with a housemate, another musician, and she explained that he had felt it right to leave the rest of his possessions to him.

A few months later that housemate, Isaac, came to visit me. In a very roundabout and gentle way, he told me that he and Greg had been a couple, and that they had been deeply in love and lived together for many years. I had known about Greg in my heart, but I had always been in denial about his homosexuality, because of all sorts of things—religion, bigotry, embarrassment, guilt. Perhaps my son distanced himself from his father and I so that we wouldn't have to face the reality of his lifestyle, which he knew would have been foreign, even incomprehensible to us. Did he fear it would have changed how we felt about him? That it would have lessened our love or our admiration? Certainly, he saved us from a painful realization, but at the same time he made us suffer something far worse. I suffered his absence almost as much as I suffered his untimely death. I learnt a lesson that day; joy and pain co-exist in every relationship, they are inseparable and complementary, we must have both. I should never have let so much distance grow between us.

The only right path lies in finding a middle ground: we must accept that life gives and takes in ways we often don't comprehend, there is so much we don't choose, but it is the only life we have and must be lived on those terms. Acceptance, that's the only road to peace. I've often asked myself what I learnt by being Greg's mother, but I've never received an answer. What I hold in my heart is his music and the memory of my beautiful little boy playing cars with his Daddy. He freely made his choice of a clean break, a life severed from ours, reserved just for him and Isaac. His father and I gave him his freedom, thinking that we were giving him what he wanted most in life. I wish it could have been different, that we had been closer, but perhaps this adversity helped him become someone stronger in his own right, as he grew into a man. Or were we just looking for an excuse—out of sight, out of mind again? Letting him go made it so much easier to avoid facing our suspicions.

I didn't listen to my son, not the way he needed me to. I confessed all of this to the young priest from Nebraska who took Padre Peter's place when he passed away, but his token words of comfort were formal and devoid of true sentiment; that boy was far from every human woe still, and could not comprehend my feelings. If he had been more mature, he could have helped me to deal with my overwhelming guilt, but it was hopeless, far beyond his realm of cognition or action. Anyone who has experienced being a parent can tell you it's not easy—it cannot be done without making mistakes. Unresolved dilemmas and deep regrets are par for the course. For example, our children feel the contrast between the values they learn from their parents and the drive of their own impulse to be themselves. We try to mold them, and they try to break the mold. It is nature's way: they must follow the pull of the tide, of their destiny. Then what? Perhaps their dreams come true, perhaps they don't—but this mechanism is hard for both sides to endure, and it is down to the intelligence of the parents to guide their offspring through it, without repressing them. Otherwise, we risk seeing them fall into patterns of destructive behavior.

Although I always pushed myself to do my best raising Greg and Resy, I can't say I'm satisfied, or even proud of myself. I can only forgive myself a little when I think that in the end everything is relative, everything is an unsolved enigma. Some cliches are true in the end; this too will pass, nothing lasts forever. Nothing, not even my century of life, lasted so very long at all. Now, talking it over with you, I finally see where Greg's path began to veer away from ours. When he realized that he wasn't quite the person that his father had imagined his son would be, that he wasn't exactly the son that this father wanted, that he wouldn't have the family his mother envisioned for him, when he started to become aware that he had a different kind of sensitivity. Irresponsibly, I didn't notice, or preferred not to notice, whether consciously or unconsciously, I kept my head in the sand. He probably thought it would be too much for me. I wish I could talk to him now, or just walk with him, along the river path in Sunset Park, holding his hand in mine once more.

CHAPTER 23

MY NAME IS LUCY, I lived on the corner of Morgan Avenue and Green River Road, in that peeling old house with the big ring of purple flowers that blooms every spring. I don't think I ever had a cozier chat than this, I feel so fuzzy and free now, I'm almost done.

Freedom is the key to everything. If we're not at liberty to be ourselves, we're not really living. Given that a truly free life demands introspection, self-examination, and self-knowledge, you must ask yourself: am I merely alive or do I actually exist? Existence implies much more than just having a pulse or a heartbeat, it means finding the courage and the desire to express all you have inside, without letting external influences throw you off course. Did I exist? I certainly tried to, albeit with fits and starts, ups and downs, full stops and dot dot dots. I endeavored to use my time well and not shy away from new things. That said, it was suffering, not novelty, that was my greatest teacher. Suffering gave me my forward momentum, driving me to live ever more intentionally year in year out. You could say we are born suffering, and yet birth is one of the most extraordinarily beautiful things a creature can experience, not just the miracle of being born, but also of giving life to another creature.

All the torment a mother suffers in childbirth disappears the very instant she feels that new life slipping out of her body. Childbirth, that exclusive indescribable miracle, makes a mother feel connected to all of creation and releases within her a unique kind of reverence, a religious sense of gratitude towards life. A life is built slowly, step by step, it's not something instant like winning the lottery. Actually, I remember my friend Bessie who kept on buying tickets in the lottery of life, obsessively trying to chase down that perfect existence, never satisfied, always bent on improving something or other. Her favorite word was "flawless." To her it was imperative to follow every rule of etiquette. Every action became progressively more premeditated, organized, and planned to perfection. But life played one of its mean tricks on her, by giving her just what she wished for: eventually Bessie's every waking moment was spent fighting to maintain a regularity and method that transformed her into a rigid, intolerant person who had no freedom at all. You couldn't ask Bessie a favor or even offer her affection; whenever she came into contact with another person, she felt overcome because she could not plan in advance for the feelings that the event would create within her.

In the end, she chose to abandon the unpredictable outside world and close herself off completely. That's how she finished up tucked away in a clinic in Boston where you can telephone her only on Tuesdays between 3 and 4 pm. Poor Bessie made herself prisoner of her own rationality, she sealed up every door that anything new and unexpected could have come in through. The unknown terrorized her, in her dreams she was lost to her obsessions so she erased even those with medication. I don't recall why I'm telling you this sad tale, when I was alive, I didn't just sit around gossiping like this, I promise you. I must have order—that's what I was trying to get at! I need to say my piece now to put it to rest forever, here in this strange place of perfect wellness I find myself in. Finally, I can put all these thoughts behind me, leaving behind my story, all neat and tidy just like my house. No more random thoughts like loose leaves blowing about in my mind. I don't think I'll be coming back to them again, and it feels lovely, I feel lighter with every word.

I know I haven't said enough about friendship, and about all the special people I encountered on my path through life. Time must be made for that, too. Friendship is a constructive element, where each is accepted for who they are. It's not a blood tie, but a second family we have freely chosen and love no holds barred. In friendship, nothing stands in the way of sincerity and tolerance, and this makes us stronger and richer. I was blessed with special friends who enriched my life. Deborah and I were at school together, she was a very beautiful girl with rare green-gold eyes and wavy blonde hair. She was popular and intelligent, but I guess she just wasn't made for following the rules. Her rebellious spirit and fiery temper often got her into trouble with the Sisters—naughtiness was not contemplated, let alone tolerated back then. Things were even worse with her father, who was an important businessman and a bit of a stuffed shirt. Deborah made quite a drama out of their arguments and spent most of her time dreaming up ways to embarrass him with one escapade or another, but she was really just a bit high strung, I think. In any case she never told me why she went to such extremes to antagonize her father. We had some wonderful adventures together, but it was never enough for her.

I suppose she simply hadn't lived enough yet to understand the consequences of her actions—all that anger she was fermenting inside her built up. It would eventually throw her off her path and, looking back, I really think she missed her destiny altogether. With seemingly scarce effort she always got good grades in school, and she was witty and well-read. Even as a schoolgirl she had an informed opinion on all the important things in life. The world was her oyster then, or so it seemed to me, and I looked up to her and admired her spunk. When we finished school, we stayed in touch and must have exchanged dozens and dozens of letters over the years. I kept them all, and decades later, when Helen read all those letters, she was amazed by how profound and insightful my seemingly nutty friend Debbie had actually been. Debbie went on to a good university and grew up to become Mrs. Deborah Leboc. Even that was a bit of a scandal because she married the acclaimed Dr Robert Leboc PhD, who had been her philosophy professor. He was much older, so perhaps it was the usual cliche of a girl searching for a father figure. They set up home and seemed to live happily together in quite a snooty neighborhood of New Harmony for many years.

Nonetheless, even after they welcomed their baby girl, Deborah somehow seemed to maintain the role of the daughter more so than the wife in their relationship. She never really decided what to do with herself and all her talent. After years dawdling through life, bored and unchallenged, a chance meeting with a Californian artist led her to abandon her sedate existence, leaving her husband and daughter to pursue him. Sadly, it was the beginning of a self-destructive decline towards an early grave. People say she became an addict and the drugs killed her, but knowing her as deeply as I did, I believe she actually overdosed on her own repressed rage, and guilt—though why her emotions had always been her poison, I never knew. Old Professor Leboc had been devastated by his wife running off, and all the usual gossip that the affair churned up but, despite the chaos, my friendship with him became much closer in that period. Although he had felt the pain of betrayal and abandonment, it had deepened his humanity rather than damaged it. Navigating his travails had honed his ability to recognize the true value of suffering as the highest teaching of life, thus he learned to live more wisely and consciously. Pain is a portal we all must cross if we strive to exist on a higher level, and he was brave enough to make that journey.

Even Don was willing to listen when Professor Leboc spoke. Though my husband was by nature generous and open, his accident had made him leery of anyone preaching at him or "doling out lessons," as he called it. He had been torn away from his first love—automobile racing—and left with a broken spirit as well as a broken body. Like all of us, he had good days and bad. Some days were cataclysmically bad—he seemed like a man waist deep in quicksand, being dragged down by the injustice of his affliction, his beleaguered existence, the random cruelty of destiny. On those days it seemed like only the Professor could help, and with guidance and gentle dialogue, Don's attitude and even his sense of humor gradually improved. There was not a trace of moralism in Leboc's words, just understanding and empathy, from man to man. It was a welcome balm for my husband's limpid, honest soul.

Leboc died a free man, he died after Deborah, and I believe he forgave her. He was free of malice, free of ego, free of shame, free of fear. He was honored as a professor and respected as a citizen and beloved father. In the years that followed, the void he left in Evansville society was filled by a literary circle and a book club organized by his faithful disciples. I often participated as a host or reader, and this helped me travel within myself and discover new things. Not long ago, I finally became conscious that being alive means possessing knowledge, of course, but it also means learning to die slowly and patiently. Death! I see him as a friend now, so often have I called out to him from the depths of my heart in the ringing silence of my bedroom. In the end he came to me painlessly, fondly, on tippy toes, careful not to startle me, moving soundlessly just like Papa and Johnny used to do, when they went out milking well before dawn. I'm getting muddled again in my tale, but I know what I'm saying. Many times, I've tried to talk about my friend death but no one listens. Whenever someone would come and visit me on the long, dark winter afternoons, I would try, but they wouldn't want to hear it.

Only Helen ever really listened, with her usual kindness and acceptance. She told me that nowadays the existence of death is not discussed in polite company—not even in hospitals. Nevertheless, it's a fact of life. We must at the very least be mindful of the reality of death. Naturally, its crudeness disturbs our illusions, clashing with the classic image of the American dream. That is the wool drawn over the eyes of the masses, to hide the existence of age, disease, pain, death. Is this how we are at the end of this millennium, drifting on obliviously, never thinking to lift our blindfolds? The bereaved, the survivors, those of us who have known the agony of losing their loved ones are kept at arm's length out of superstition. It's easier to talk about death as something we only read about in the newspapers, rather than what it really should represent for everyone: a vital moment of spiritual awakening. When someone elderly passes away, we experience it hurriedly, with a few trite phrases and a hypocritical, briskly executed funeral void of any true meaning. The goal is not to honor the life of the departed, but to ward off the full impact of the meaning of their death for ourselves.

On the contrary, my ancestors believed that you could tell a lot about how a man had lived by attending his funeral. My grandparents and my parents always respected the traditional process for mourning a loved one. Grieving was part of a deeply moving ritual that typically lasted three days, with the laying out of the deceased, the rites, the choosing of flowers, and the wake. The words to be said were carefully written and recited; the best memories, the happiest moments, with examples of time spent together fruitfully, time invested, time given freely, time treasured. Too few people follow this tradition nowadays, not realizing that they are depriving themselves of the chance to benefit from the lessons to be learned from the life of the deceased and from the memories of their time on earth—wisdom which could otherwise be conserved and woven into their lives and the fabric of their community, reinforcing it. Ultimately, we must attribute value and meaning to all of life's events, and every single expression of humanity, death included.

Accepting and loving the gift of life with full consciousness, with all its inevitable pains and pleasures, necessitates accepting and loving the idea of death, too. I don't suppose I'll be in any condition for a wake by the time they find me.

CHAPTER 24

I'M LUCY. I'VE TOLD my name to every cloud in the sky by now. I wish someone would close my eyes. No one is coming. I wonder if I'm lost. But no, I'm in my rocker like a baby, my dead body is drying out, and my consciousness is separating from it. The facts are clear to me now.

I think my poor old TV has been on this whole time. What if it's been going three days non-stop? I hope it won't overheat and burn the house down before Helen gets here. She must save the books and the photographs, at least the framed ones, and the cherry pie. Will my trusted television transform my home into my funeral pyre? That would be a funny ending, worthy of the worst airport novel! My books were good company, but as I grew older and my eyes weaker, the television became my best friend. It evoked such sweet memories for me, reruns of old shows and my favorite black & white movies—anything with Fred and Ginger would always perk me right up. Most of all it was undemanding company to drink my morning coffee with as I watched the weather forecast and the local news. So, all things considered, I loved my television, but I was no fool and I knew I couldn't just surrender to it. It's not bad by nature, but it has to be managed is all, just like the cookie jar or the honey pot. It's too tempting otherwise; it can suck your time away hour after hour, as you watch someone else's life unfold. It actually seems to trick your brain into thinking you're really doing something, not just vegetating on the sofa, or even worse, in your bed. Like with so many things, if you're not the boss of it, then it's the boss of you.

The immense power that TV news has on families today is something that has been worrying me for decades. News travels at the speed of light now, no more pony post. Where is the time for reflection, for letting the shock of the new information sink in—how can we genuinely understand a situation instead of succumbing to the pressure to instantly surrender to our gut reactions? Everything devours itself. Everything moves so quickly, leaving us feeling incomplete, confused, inadequate, somehow ashamed that our comparatively dull wits can't keep up with the speed and complexity of the electronic world. But human beings are not meant to live like lightning bolts. We are meant to exist in communities, we are meant to blossom in nature, we prosper through togetherness practiced over time. A garden doesn't grow as a gut reaction, a vegetable patch isn't planted in a moment of fear or mistrust or frenzy that blinds us to the beauty and bounty will that come. Life must be nurtured on its own terms, in its own time, following its own rules. Nature has its own special calendar and order. A seed must be buried in damp soil and given enough warmth so it can split open its husk and sprout upwards. The sapling it becomes needs light to grow, just like the seed needed darkness. People are the same, the different stages of our lives follow an unalterable sacred procession that we are put here on earth to benefit from and to rejoice in, not to toy with.

I understand little of technology—I'm embarrassed to say I never even learned to use a typewriter properly, let alone a computer, but I know that machine will change the world. What about the children of today—so absorbed, so preoccupied by entertainment without any educational value, or worse, with gratuitous violence—will they be able to build their own logical and emotional parameters, to cobble together a framework for their own development using such flimsy, fallacious materials as these? Life has taught me that what matters most is the value we ascribe to our actions and communicate to others, but this value surfaces only after a long process of reflection and sedimentation. The eye-popping speed of the modern world is blurring this natural pathway to wisdom. What does this frantic future hold? It's an open question, or worse vain rhetoric you'll say, at this late stage. Nonetheless, I reserve the right, even now in my final moments, to a twinge of anxiety when I consider our future. The massive changes that are needed demand an equally massive political about-turn. A reversal of the behavior and mentality of the current powers that be. The development of new technology must not be allowed to suffocate or disintegrate individuals. Infants have a right to grow at their own pace, as nature intended. Children's creativity is vital to their development, while staring passively at screens deprives them of developing their own physical and mental space, they rarely get the chance to use imagination in their play.

The twentieth century may soon seem like the last age of innocence, in spite of the tide of vice that rose around it, because it seems to me that we are seeing the extinction of the last truly wild, free human specimens. So few people even remember first-hand what mankind was like, before we finally became fully domesticated and lost touch with our most instinctive, spiritual and ancestral parts. Where are they now; the Shawnee, the Delaware, the Potawatomie, the tribes that were as intrinsic to my homeland as its earth, air and water? Their undoing was also our own. Nothing lasts. What came before? I remember visiting the Angel Mounds with Don, many years ago, when they opened the new visitor center. I guess we were both retired by then, because we spent the whole day just wandering about the gigantic ancient site. Tens of thousands of people must have lived there once, like us they settled snug in the embrace of the river, but now they are gone.

Nevertheless, the obstinate pioneer in me is still hoping to wake up to a new frontier, perhaps in a different dimension. I hope that new elements will come to restore balance in this world. Afterall, we are protected by the great miracle of our Creator, so everything must eventually return to the middle ground, the rut, the furrow we are destined to plow. That is where the path of wisdom and balance lies, though access is strictly reserved for those willing to shoulder the responsibility of shepherding mankind through its continual evolution. I've have seen many lives go off the rails, but I have also experienced the secret joy of knowing that those lives, too, had meaning, because seeded a fruitful fear in us. They obliged us to transform that fear into motivation, and new, urgent reasons to improve, to better ourselves even. The negative is compost for the positive: we ferment and grow more potent through trials and suffering. What happens in private will happen in public too; the media will eventually have to find proper guidance and acquire moderation and respect for ethics. *Solo dosis facit venenum.* The dose makes the poison as said the old adage goes—it's such a shame that nobody studies Latin anymore, it helps you make sense of so many things. That which is unbalanced is also necessarily precarious and impermanent. That which is excessive and extreme eventually crumbles, burns out, and is carried away by the same ill wind that once fanned its flames: it is a law written in stone, in land, in water, in those silent unmoving mounds that persist throughout history.

Where am I? I really hope someone will tell me what's going on soon. It seems like I'm floating, suspended in time, while everything that was once inside me drains out into this story, the story of my life, or of any life, even of life in general, I suppose. There's no melodrama thankfully, and no spectators. My heart is light and it's releasing everything it ever held, everything that was still interwoven, embroidered into this world, has been minutely unpicked. Billions of tiny hands at work within me, I feel them all, and I know I am almost all undone. This physical existence will soon be no more. I don't believe in coincidences. It's odd what happened three days ago, when I lay back on this chair and began to fade. That afternoon Helen had come to say goodbye before she left for a trip, and later on, Mary, who always stopped by twice a day for my meals and my pills, had called to say she was coming down with a fever and would send someone else to look in on me. Despite my aches and pains, I could still walk and get to the bathroom, and fend for myself in the kitchen as far as making a sandwich or heating up some soup went, so I wasn't worried. But somehow as I shuffled out of my robe, I felt that my big day had come. Looking in the mirror, I combed my hair carefully, and even thought of putting on a touch of lipstick. In some strange way, it seemed important to make the extra effort.

CHAPTER 25

DYING ALONE WAS BIZARRE and wildly improbable, especially given all the people that could have happened across me at any moment. Helen was away on a trip, but there should have been Mary like always, and Dr. Santoro had said he would call me every day while I was home alone. After Helen left, a short circuit blew out the phonelines at the clinic. At the same time Mary was realizing far too late that she didn't in fact have a simple fever. I have this knowledge here in the place I am now. I don't know how I know, or why; perhaps something has been seeping into my consciousness as my story has been spilling out. What poor Mary had thought was just a cold was in fact the first murmur of a heart attack. I hope the ambulance made it to her on time. Dr Santoro, being unable to telephone, made a mental note to try again later, but one urgent patient after another kept him busy. The next day, since I wasn't answering, and he couldn't leave the clinic to check on me himself, he called Sheriff Hobson and asked him to stop by if he could. And so Gerald Hobson is destined to finally discover me on the third day.

That's alright by me, he's a good boy, I hope I won't frighten him too much. He's always run off his feet, you know, and he must be nearing pension age by now. They're understaffed at the station, but he's a hard worker and I'm certain he'll make time to call in to see me on his way to work or on his way home. He'll set his alarm ten minutes earlier if needs be, he won't forget me, that's just how he was raised, you see. I taught his mother for many years, and she used to bring him to me from time to time, to help with him with his homework and to try to instill some French in him. I'd see her combing his hair down in the car before she brought him in; she set him up for life as well as she could. My body isn't much decomposed thanks to the air conditioning. I left the house spruce and tidy as always. My rose petal potpourri hangs sweet in the air of the hallway. My body is snug in the lovely rocker we bought from the Amish several eons back. Everything is in its proper place, only my soul is missing. Now it's here in this new place, somewhere totally indescribable, and I am finally on a real adventure, a voyage, a journey of discovery.

Here all the things that were unknown are known, and there is a new unknown that is so much vaster than anything I could ever have imagined. Gerald will be the one to find me today, and I'm curious to see what it will be like when he crosses the threshold. There is a coyness, a bashfulness in death, that I wasn't expecting. I am leaving life and going off to make a new marriage with infinity. We are born, we grow, live, love, work, procreate, pray, push another bead of the rosary through our fingers. The rosary of life is a continual, repeating gift and then one day we die, and that too is gift. To go with a certain levity into this new dimension, this great void that we seek to fill, takes presence and preparation. After all this talking I'm ready now, nothing is keeping me here any longer. In a sense I have been preparing for this next step since the day I was born. Gerald will be my escort, my chaperon—a strapping lad in uniform, brave of spirit and kind of heart, how fortunate I am! I have no more questions, nothing to reveal, I have revisited good times and bad, moments that made this life what it was. I was fortunate indeed; I lived in a place that I loved, that I belonged to, that belonged to me—my beloved Evansville, Indiana. I'm ready to move on now.

So, these are my few, simple secrets that I pass on to you. I leave behind some shreds of existence, a love story, my lessons, my regrets laid to rest, my hopes for what's to come. I loved my family, I accepted the pain of knowing I would not share in the life of my children as they grew into adults, and of not growing old with them nearby. I passionately loved my husband, the only man I ever knew intimately. I admired his enthusiasm for life. As much as I was irked by his fiery nature, I also appreciated and strove to emulate that ardor, because I envied his thirst for the life of the flesh. Eventually I managed to put that envy to good use and be motivated by it. I came to understand his suffering and his struggle to create a new identity for himself when his body was transformed so brutally. This knowledge helped me to be a good companion even as the years blunted my femininity. Most of all it stood me in good stead towards the end, when my crumbling secular exterior became modified to the extent that I sometimes got quite a start when I looked in the mirror. I was a dutiful worker, maybe I could have done more, but my home life rightly absorbed a lot of my energy. I cultivated friendships that filled my heart.

I built a loving home and shared it. I planted a garden that gave sustenance and shelter. I was kind to animals. I studied, and prayed, and strived earnestly to reach full maturity in my final years, letting go of many petty vanities. I finally saw the teaching and the grand design, even behind the worst misfortunes that struck me. I received much good and gave it back, and I delighted constantly in the beauty of creation. Thank you, I appreciate everything, every instant. Thank you and thank you again—thank you God!

CHAPTER 26

WHAT BEAUTIFUL MUSIC, IT reminds me . . . it reminds me of when my Don used to sing to me. The light is getting stronger and clearer at last. I hear something . . . like cheering, clapping . . .

Suddenly I feel energy running through me, I think I'm finally going to wake up! I'm warm and tingling. The sound is getting closer to me, or is my heart swelling up so big that I'm actually growing nearer to it? The light is shining from inside me now, pulsating, getting brighter by the second. I am all light. Ah there's such a sweet smell in the air— something I haven't smelt for years, like a meadow of wild flowers swaying in the summer breeze. I'm not indoors anymore, I'm leaving, rising up like the sun. I can see better now, there are shapes in the distance. Who is it? I'm nearly there, they're reaching out to me! I hear voices. Someone is calling my name over and over again. Oh my God! Don . . . is that you, my love? I'm coming Resy, Greg, Mama, Papa, all of you . . . Oh! All my people, all my loves, all my heart, all my home . . .

Oh my God, what bliss!

CHAPTER 27

WHEN SHERIFF HOBSON BURST breathlessly through the kitchen door, he didn't quite know what to expect, but it certainly wasn't anything like what he found. The scene was one of almost surreal calm and order. He crossed the threshold haltingly, suppressing a fleeting urge to apologize for the abrupt intrusion. "Ma'am? Miss Belmont? Lucy? Is anyone home?" he called out . . . but his voice didn't travel, it just hung brittle in the crisp, sweet air. Everything was in its place as always, the sink was empty, a single pristine cup and saucer on the drying rack. He hadn't been inside for many years, but nothing had changed, the kitchen must have been fifty years old, but still good as knew he thought. The linoleum floor made almost no sound under his feet, he felt like a fisherman waist-deep in a river, wading through decades past. The television was on in the living-room, and it kept him company as made his way upstairs.

Lucy gave him quite a start as he entered the bedroom. She was sitting up quite straight, neatly dressed, a woolen blanket demurely tucked around her lap, rocking almost imperceptibly in her usual spot by the window. He let out an involuntary little yelp and then felt sheepish. He knew instantly that she was dead, but for a moment she seemed to rock towards him, eyes wide open, and he had to restrain himself from reaching for her. After he'd called dispatch, he realized he didn't feel right leaving her all alone in the bedroom again, it didn't seem polite.

She was always so neat and particular—he felt awkward, messy. He took off his hat and ran his fingers through his hair, then put it back on carefully. He wished he had a tie to straighten, but he wasn't wearing his dress uniform, so he just smoothed down his shirt front and positioned himself as unobtrusively as possible. He stayed by her side and spoke gently to her as they waited, although he knew logically that it was far too late. "I'm so sorry I didn't get here sooner Miss Belmont, but I'm here now, and I'll take care of you," he murmured almost shyly, "I won't leave you; I'll make sure everything is done right and proper, just like you would have wanted."

Outside, in a circle, all the irises were blooming.

Postscript

AND SO HERE WE are, dear reader, at the end of the story of Lucy Belmont, or perhaps this is just the beginning. As I told you at the outset, this meandering tale sat for about two decades at the bottom of my desk drawer, until one fine day in early 2020. During the long months of forced reclusion, while the whole world was shut down, I finally got around to some tidying and I came across it again. Something made me take the dusty manuscript in hand and start reading. Page after page I consumed voraciously, as if I was encountering the story for the first time. By chapter 3 I had the pleasant perception of visiting with a distant relative I hadn't seen in a very long time. The heroine, Lucy, with her ninety-seven years of humble, everyday existence, photographed the fearsome beauty of a particular phase of modern American society. She had been born into a nation in evolution, at a time of exponential technological development—an age of miracles.

By chapter 10 I realized that this story was both very ordinary and very extraordinary. Lucy's little world was firmly encased in what we call "the American dream," and this simple account, that sprung up in my heart so mysteriously, was somehow like a hologram or a fly caught in amber. Fossilized within it lay a crucial historical and anthropological reflection of the thundering avalanche of progress that the United States underwent in a single, revolutionary century. The American dream enticed many millions of adventurers from war torn Europe to strike out for the new world. This new international human community, of which our Lucy Belmont was a result, was founded on the ability of each member of that cultural melting pot to adapt their own roots and traditions, while conserving what was sane and healthy. Like those rights and responsibilities bound to the principle of liberty, America is living proof of a wild idea; that the pursuit of happiness itself can become the uniting aspiration of all peoples, for all times. And what is meant by the word happiness if not family, safety, dignity, independence and faith in the future? Of course, the future is a trail that must be blazed before it can be followed *en masse*, blazed by those brave-hearted mavericks ready to risk everything to make a dream come true.

The American experience helps us understand the complex phenomenon of immigration, which is overwhelming my home in Europe and much of the western world currently. Civilizations can be positively transformed by immigration when a healthy balance is maintained. Conversely, when the interactions between the native civilization and the newcomers are not properly dosed and supported, society implodes and instability pervades, bringing regression. It will take many decades to regain the human qualities and sensitivities that we had established. What relief can we find in Lucy's small world for immense, global issues? We might take a leaf from her book, try to dream up a positive vision of the future, and put a different spin on the negatives we encounter, even when dealing with epochal disruption, whether from uncontrolled mass immigration or uncontrollable new technology. Lucy saw some unimaginable transformations, yet she managed to curate her existence, and cultivate the values she bore in her ancestral blood, she drew nourishment from her roots, and watered the seeds of good in herself and all around her. Her values were the compass that guided her to her place in heaven. Now that this river of words has run its course, all that remains on its dry bed is the question; looking at the values we have chosen to nurture—where is our compass leading us?

This book is dedicated to everyone who strives to live respecting the greater values. With sincere thanks to Dario, Emily, Giorgio, Louise, Lucia, Matt, and Savanah.

Luisella Traversi Guerra
Bergamo, April 8, 2024.

Acknowledgments

THIS BOOK OWES A debt to four very special texts which, through words and images, emboldened and embellished the story of Lucy Belmont. Collected by the author in the 1990s, the first was the fascinating and tender treasure, *Green River Road—From Cornfields to Concrete*, written by the gifted and talented fifth graders of the Hebron Elementary School in Evansville, Indiana, and their teacher Libby Culiver. Another deeply impactful book was *The Angel and the Serpent—the Story of New Harmony,* by the infinitely poetic author William E. Wilson, which provided an enchanting glimpse into the complex hearts and minds of the Harmonists. Thirdly Darrel Bigham, then professor of history at the University of Southern Indiana, offered a hypnotic collection of period photographs capturing every imaginable detail of public and private life in the Evansville Region; the Tri-State of southwestern Indiana, western Kentucky, and southern Illinois, as it was in the 1800s, in his publication: *Images of America—Evansville*. Coincidentally, he also inspired Libby Culiver to create the aforementioned *Green River Road—From Cornfields to Concrete* as a teaching tool. Lastly, the Historic Preservation Committee of the Junior League of Evansville, aided by contributions from the Willard Library and many local citizens, compiled *Reflections Upon a Century of Architecture, Evansville, Indiana*, in which each of the historical district's magnificent edifices are brought to life so charmingly.

In gratitude for these four books that lit the fuse of the author's imagination and allowed her beloved Lucy to burst forth onto the page.

Margaret Louise Fitzgibbon

www.ingramcontent.com/pod-product-compliance
Lightning Source LLC
Chambersburg PA
CBHW060426260626
47161CB00005B/1801

* 9 7 9 8 3 8 5 2 2 3 6 0 2 *